CHAIRMAN OF THE BOARD

CHAIRMAN OF THE BOARD

A NOVELLA BY
PERRY SLAUGHTER

SINISTER REGARD
New York
2014

ISBN 978-1-941-92805-9

Trade paperback edition: December 2014

www.sinisterregard.com
www.perryslaughter.com

For her

CHAIRMAN OF THE BOARD

I

SATURDAY NIGHT

"Okay, we have our question. Who will be the next politician in space?"

Gauzy white trails climbing lazily to the ceiling: smoke from a dozen joints scribbles its signature into the harsh pool of light. Bodies around the dining room table tense in concentration.

"R . . . A . . ."

The chorus of hoarse teenaged voices calls out each letter as it comes up, the flat wooden pointer beneath their stained fingers gliding at random inside the ouija board's half-circle of alphabet. Fingers of rain drum against the window, as if eager to join in the game. Depeche Mode try in vain to shout them down from their prison in the corner speakers, and the resonant bass vibrates the table and sets the pretzel crumbs to dancing on the carpet. On the wide-screen TV jammed between a pair of fraying armchairs, a quartet of innocent and bare-assed young blossoms cavort blithely through the dappled light of a forest glen, but their gymnastics go unheeded.

". . . Y . . . G . . ."

Sam is wedged tight into the ring of bodies, the reek of beer, weed, and cheap perfume heavy in his nostrils. Water spots on his wire-rimmed glasses smudge his vision, and limp strands of brown hair tickle his eyelids. His simple blue jeans and checked shirt set him apart from the eclectic mix of studded leather and bold designer fashions that circle the table; he is the outsider. He has one reluctant fingertip on the pointer, against his better judgment.

"... U ... N ... Raygun!"

Laughter gushes up orgasmically, and the circle widens a little as hands come off the pointer. "Raygun?" Sam demands of Corman, across the table. "What the hell's *that* supposed to mean?"

Corman Kendricksen tents his fingers and lean on his elbows, radiating calm. He's the only one besides Sam who has not touched the booze or the drugs; he's also the only one with a chair. A pair of razor-nailed hands, not his own, crawl over his shoulders, flit past his bolo tie, and dart inside his shirt. The laughter degenerates into a series of low giggles, music boiling into the gaps like electronic caulk. "The board can't spell worth a shit. It means *Ronnie* Raygun, our beloved Commander-in-Space—uh, I mean Chief."

The laughter erupts anew, wilder than before, and Sam's mouth quirks involuntarily. But it doesn't smile.

Corman tilts his head back to accept a slow kiss from the girl they call Nymph, and her silver-tipped nails glide up his neck, through his mousse-lacquered hair. Hands are playfully errant all around the table; Sam swats at one that alights on his buttock, regretfully.

Three sharp raps on the ceiling. Giggling faces turn upward, like expectant acolytes listening for a voice from heaven. But the voice they get comes from the master bedroom upstairs, angry, muffled, and unintelligible. "Settle down up there," Corman yells at the ceiling. "We're trying to have a party!" The room dissolves into hysterics, and the upstairs grumbling loses out to the din. "My old man," Corman stage-whispers to Sam. "Just reminding us to save him some dope."

Sam glances around the room, at the stereo equipment, at Corman's natty get-up, then up at the cracked and peeling ceiling, and wonders, not for the first time, how they can afford it all.

Corman clears his throat. "All right, sports fans, lemme have your undivided attention for a few moments." Hand snaking up the smooth plain of Nymph's belly. "The next question is dedicated to our guest of honor, my friend . . . Sammy *Pauling*"—his best Ed McMahon enthusiasm—"who's keeping me afloat this quarter in Pascal and keeping me from snagging the big F in Ol' Lady Finch's class. Let's have a hand!" Sporadic applause starts up, then quickly peters out. Someone claps Sam on the back. He smiles weakly; the evening's truce between hacker and hipsters in an uneasy one at best.

"Now, as we all know, Sam's the captain of our illustrious Buchanan High School chess team, who open their season this Monday with a crucial match against—"

"It's just an exhibition match . . . ," Sam says tentatively.

"Even so, it'll set the tone for the rest of the season to come. Now, I've got a little wager riding on this, so I'm curious. Gather 'round!" The circle tightens up, and everyone puts a finger or two on the pointer, including Sam. He's interested in this one, despite himself.

"Okay, ready? Here's the question. Will our good buddy Sammy checkmate his worthy opponent on Monday?"

The pointer slides. "c . . . o . . . n . . . s . . . e . . . e . . . d . . . e . . . d . . ."

"Ha-ha!" Corman exclaims. "It concedes. You're in like Flynn, Sammy-boy." He grab's Sam's hand and pumps it vigorously. "C'ratulations. You're gonna make me a very rich man." The partiers cheer.

"But Corman," Sam protests, "that might mean—"

But he is ignored. "*I think it's telling you you're* conceited," says Nymph, tickling Corman's ear with her lips. Her husky voice surprises Sam every time she speaks; he sees her type as no more than mute—read *dumb*—and slavishly affectionate sex-toys. Something you can get cheaper in a vending machine in Las Vegas.

Sam tries to frame his comment again, but the clamor and din drown him out. Corman taps the pointer, and it quivers in response. "Okay, okay, kids," he says, spreading his arms wide and leaning back in his chair. Nymph's hands help to keep him balanced. "Who's got another question for the Chairman of the Board?"

A tall girl with stubble for eyebrows speaks out over the others, where Sam could not. "Corm-man, I want to know what this joker here"—she plucks a hairy hand from her breast and mashes it fondly in her own—"*really* does for kicks when I'm not around." She brings the hand to her mouth; her tongue dances around its fingertips.

The partiers giggle, and someone shouts, "Buss-*ted!*" Sam backs up a step, almost out of the light, and tries not to look toward the kitchen door and the rolling free rain-slick suburban hills beyond.

Corman's eyes crinkle and he rocks back down onto all fours. "Looks like Jen may have some sort of a grievance here, kids," he says. "Let's see if we can't straighten it out for her. Fingers off the flesh and onto the planchette!"

The circle contracts as everyone strains to get a finger on the pointer, even Jen's beau—though it seems to Sam that the boy is sweating a little more heavily than the others. Sam takes another step back, wiping his glasses on his shirttail, and the flickering darkness swallows him up.

"Our question is this," Corman intones, closing his eyes. Nymph's pale, thin hand brackets his on the surface of the pointer. "How does our friend Moose here get off when he doesn't have Jenny to screw him silly?"

The pointer slides around indecisively for a moment on its three stubby legs, as if weighed down by the dozens of fingers on its back. Then it zigs sluggishly across the board to the letter M. A crease splits Corman's brow. He surveys the circle fixedly while the pointer moves weakly in another direction and stops. Voices mutter. Moose exhales audibly. "Sam?" Corman calls. "Where'd you go?"

All heads swivel and Sam freezes. Light reflects coldly from his glasses; the speakers grind out an accusatory synthesized riff. "I—uh, have to take a piss." The girls onscreen behind him seem to echo his sentiments.

"That can wait, Sammy," says Corman suavely. "We need you. The board won't put out without you. See, it's not doing a damn thing."

Sam hovers on the edge of bolting for the back door. These aren't the friendliest faces he has ever known. He wonders how far he can get, how hyped they really are. He wonders if it's worth finding out.

Nymph, with her black lipstick and Egyptian-style eyeliner, pouts at him seductively—her wide dark eyes nonetheless ambiguous. "C'mon, Sam. Come on back. You don't want to spoil the party."

Faces around the circle murmur and nod their agreement. Even the music pauses momentarily, as if to second her plea. The rain pounds on. With a score or more eyes tugging in silence, Sam's shoulders slump and he returns to the table. They clear a space for him, opposite Corman and Nymph. He locks eyes with Corman and adds his finger to the others resting lightly on the pointer.

As he touches it, it jumps, as if receiving an electric shock. Eyes widen and breath is indrawn. The game resumes.

"M . . . A . . ." The end of Moose's joint glows cherry-red, and his forehead gleams like polished chrome. ". . . S . . . T . . . E . . ." He can't wipe away the sweat, for he has one hand on the pointer and Jen imprisons the other. Sam feels an urge to reach out and wipe it away for him. ". . . R . . . B . . . A . . ." A nervous jet of foul smoke shoots into the center of the ring. Sam's eyes water. ". . I . . . T . . ."

The pointer grinds to a halt. "That's it," Corman says, grinning cruelly. "Master-bait."

Moose snatches his hand back from the pointer as if from a flame, as the jeers and catcalls fall about him. Whether from anger or embarrassment Sam cannot tell, but his face matches the color of the sizzling ash he still puffs. The abuse does not let up, and even Jen is laughing heartlessly. Moose's features harden; he whips the joint from his mouth and grinds it out in the palm of his hand. His lips tremble. A faint, sickening odor fills the air, and the voices fall silent. "Hey, Moose," says Jen softly, taking the spent butt away from him. "None of that, 'kay? It's just a joke."

"I'll kill him," he mutters, not looking her in the eye. The music thunders, nearly drowning out his words, and the room tenses.

Jen lays one hand on his shoulder and lifts his chin with the other. "You're stoned, man. Don't get yourself worked up. Try to laugh. C'mon, sweet."

"I'll kill him."

"Listen to me. It's only a joke. No one takes any of this seriously." She glares at the cluster of frozen kids. "Do you? You don't really take any of this seriously. You *know* it's only a joke."

No one says a word. No one looks at her. Guilt and nausea clutch at Sam's stomach. He wishes he'd taken off when he had the chance.

"It's not a joke, Jenny," Moose says thickly. His fists are clenched and hang like maces at the ends of his arms. "It's not a joke anymore."

Tears bulge in the corners of Jen's eyes. "Don't do this to yourself. Please."

Corman chuckles. "It's probably better than doing it with you, babe."

Moose whirls and the maces swing. Observers scatter. "Don't!" Jen shouts, and Nymph hurls herself in front of Corman. The blow stops short of its target. Jen takes Moose's arm. Corman is smiling broadly, imperturbably. "You fucking bastard," Jen hisses. "You really did deserve that."

Face twisting, Corman stands up. "You want your so-called man there to kill someone so badly? Well, in that case we'll *find* someone for him to kill!" He slaps his hands down onto the pointer. "Whom does Moose have our permission to kill?" he sputters. Nothing happens. "Damn it all, Sam, get over here."

Sam's head is spinning. With such a sudden change in Corman's demeanor, he doesn't dare to hesitate. Spots swimming before his eyes, Sam crosses to Corman's side and sets his fingers on the pointer. Nymph smiles at him weakly, touches both their hands. Her fingers are as cool as milk.

"B . . . ," Corman reads, half shouting the letters, "I, R, D . . . L, A, Y, D, I, E. There, Moose, the board says there's some poor old lady selling popcorn for the pigeons out in the city park who you can kill if you need to, but don't try pulling any of that shit on me or you'll regret it." He flings himself into his chair, and the pale, thin hands begin to massage his temples. The dozen or so onlookers whisper among themselves, letting go an occasional nervous laugh. Jen leads a sullen Moose to one of the darkened corners of the room and tries to soothe him. Sam doesn't understand why they don't leave.

His own throat itches from the smoke; he'd kill for a good, cold Coke. But all the partiers can offer him is coke, in dusty lower-case.

"Come on, gang, lighten up," Corman says, wriggling under Nymph's ministrations. "This is still a party, and the best part's yet to come, bad pun. It's time to play Match Game!"

A ragged, half-hearted cheer goes up, and the partiers reform their circle around the table. Sam figures now would be a good time to slip away, but Nymph is keeping an eye on him. He doesn't dare to move.

"All right," says Corman, "we've got roughly the same number of each sex here. Which of the guys wants to be first?" Every male hand goes up. "Okay, Scott, you were first. You got it. Put your fingers on the planchette." A boy with asymmetrical blond hair reaches out a hand. "C'mon, Sam, we need your help, too."

Sam dry-swallows and touches the pointer.

"Great. Now . . . let's make this boy a match!"

Without hesitation, the pointer spells out DARRLEEN. "Hot *shit!*" Scott exclaims. A blush steals across the face of one of the girls in circle, one Sam thinks could be very pretty with a decent hairdo and about one-quarter the makeup. But the appeal of her body is inarguable. She and Scott slip into a corner, their figures set a-flicker by erotic pulses of light from the television.

"Keep your arms and legs inside at all times and have fun," Corman says. "Okay, so who's next?"

Two by two, the ouija board pairs them up, until the only ones left are Corman, Nymph, and Sam. "Well, sorry, Sammy, but it looks like you're out of luck tonight."

"It's just as well. I've really got to be—"

"Do him anyway, Corm," says Nymph suddenly. She shrugs weakly under Corman's questioning gaze. "Just for the hell of it."

A slow smile spreads over Corman's features. "All right, just for the hell of it. Fingers, Sam. Okay, great. Now, who should our good buddy Sam be spending the rest of the night with?"

The pointer traces out its zig-zagging path, while Corman keeps track of the letters. "K, A, I, T . . . F, I, T, S . . . Y, O, U." He turns to Nymph, chuckling with evident relief, and runs a finger down her cheek. "Did you hear that, babe? Kate Fitzhugh, of all people. The damn thing's got Sammy matched up with Miss Congeniality of Buchanan High School. What do you think of that, Sam . . . ? Hey, Sammy . . . ? Where the hell . . . ?"

Only the electric-blue flickerings answer him, from the four naughty girls who seem to coordinate all the room's activity.

II

SUNDAY MORNING

"Sam." A voice echoing out from reality to the far edge of curved dreamspace. "Wake up, son. The phone's for you."

One bleary eye pries itself open. His mother stands in the doorway, her starch-white nurse's uniform rumpled and wrinkled from sleep. "All right," he croaks, wiping his eyes. Sunlight the color of pus bleeds in through the thin curtains over his bed, stains the sheets in shades of sickness. His mouth tastes like soggy cardboard. "I've got it." His fingers quest blindly across the desktop adjacent to the bed, past the computer keyboard to knock the receiver from its cradle in the obsidian-black answering machine. "Hello?"

Dial tone. "Other phone," says his mother, rolling her eyes. "The computer phone. It's Donny Phu. Eight-thirty, like he said."

"Oh, yeah." He sits up, runs his fingers through his hair, and answers line two, his private unlisted number. "Morning, Donny." Mrs. Pauling exits, pulling the door softly shut behind her, a half-formed smile on her lips.

"Hi, Sam!" Even by phone, the voice is thin, whimpery, and

obnoxious. "Ready to play?"

Sam sighs. "Yeah, I guess. How do you want to run it?"

"I've already got Chesster booted over here, so we can run it from my machine and do the bulletin board in parallel from yours."

"Okay. Lemme get booted up. It'll be a couple of minutes. Twelve hundred baud, right?"

"Yeah."

Sam climbs wearily out of bed, massaging his eyelids. He flips on the modem behind his PC, drops the receiver into place, and selects two diskettes from the clutter atop his desk. With the disks slotted, he boots up the machine, brings the modem online, and types a brief command: B:BULBOARD.EXE

825-3847 ONLINE, the computer informs him after a moment.

ALL SET, DONNY, he types.

GREAT, is the reply. HERE COMES CHESSTER.

The top three-quarters of Sam's screen blanks out, to be replaced by the eight-by-eight grid of a chessboard. Donny's PC randomly assigns Sam the first move. He toggles from bulletin-board mode to chess and opens with the king's pawn. Donny matches him, and a line of characters winks across the bottom of the screen. NERVOUS FOR MONDAY?

Sam advances his bishop, then toggles. HELL NO. WE'RE GOING TO KICK ASS. He breathes thanks that the bulletin board can't transmit the false bravado behind his prediction.

RIGHT ON! WESTMORELAND IS DOG FOOD. Donny's knight moves into a block.

DAMN YOU, types Sam. Now he can't move his knight into position.

GET REAL. YOU DIDN'T EXPECT ME TO FALL FOR THAT. WE'RE IN SERIOUS TRAINING HERE.

The game continues for several minutes, interspersed with banal small talk, and neither player gains much ground. At last Sam manages to trap one of Donny's crafty bishops. GET OUT OF THAT IF YOU CAN.

Donny stalls. HARVEY JONES WANTS TO COME OVER THIS EVENING FOR SOME PRACTICE BEFORE THE MATCH, he taps out. It is a diversion ploy; Sam spots the rook moving in on his flank. WILL YOU BE AVAILABLE THEN?

He blocks with a pawn. NICE TRY. AND NO, I CAN'T PLAY TONIGHT.

WHY NOT?

I'M GOING OUT.

WHERE?

Sam sighs in exasperation. His hacker friends are nice guys, but have no sense of discretion. TO A PLAY, he answers reluctantly.

WHAT PLAY?

Sam groans. His eyeballs hurt. YOU'VE NEVER HEARD OF IT, TRUST ME.

WELL, WHO ARE YOU GOING WITH?

JUST MOVE, DONNY. IT'S NOT IMPORTANT.

IS IT A DATE?

OK, IT'S A DATE.

NO SHIT? WITH A GIRL? WHO?

The phone jangles and Sam jumps, then breathes a sigh of relief. It's the other line, the one with the answering machine he shares with his mother. "Hello," he says, cradling the receiver under his chin.

"Hey, Sam. It's Roger. What's up?"

"Headache, that's what." Awkwardly, he types as he talks: GOT A PHONE CALL, DONNY. SAVE GAME. I'LL CALL BACK. Then he turns off the PC. "What do you need?"

"Tried calling you last night, but you weren't home. Out with the chess team?" Roger's voice rolls smoothly across the line, a reflection of his personality.

"No, I was at a party."

"A party? Whose— Wait, you didn't go to Kendricksen's party, did you? What did I tell you about—"

"You're not my mother, Rog," says Sam defiantly. "And anyway, you don't know Corman to judge him. He's really not that bad. I was there all night, and he didn't touch a bit of marijuana, or even any beer."

"But there *was* beer and marijuana there, you admit."

"Cocaine, too, I think. A couple of the kids got nosebleeds."

"God, Sam," Roger sighs, "I really don't understand you sometimes. You're so concerned about your image, and then you start hanging out with the druggies. Pretty soon you're going to have a reputation."

Sam shoots to his feet. A pain stabs through his head, and he realizes he doesn't have his glasses on. Hasn't had all morning. "Are you worried about my reputation? Really and truly? 'Cause I heard something last night that makes me wonder."

Roger says nothing. The moment stretches like elastic, until Sam gives in and continues:

"Corman knows about me and Kate."

More silence. "So?" says Roger at last. "You think I told him or what? I thought we were best friends, Sam. Best friends don't tell secrets like that, and they sure as hell don't make those kinds of accusations."

"Well, who else . . . ?" Sam says with waning self-confidence.

"Maybe Kate talks about you to her friends. Ever consider that?"

"But Rog . . ."

"I know. She's a special girl and you don't want anyone think-ing you and her are doing anything untoward. You don't want her getting that kind of a rep. But Sam, you and her keep see-ing each other and there's no way it can stay a secret. And then you're going to have to take some responsibility for seeing that none of those rumors can get started, that there's no reason for them to get started. And all you need right now is for people to start hearing that you're running around with the Kendricksen crowd. Kate's a fragile girl, man. Guys have hurt her before, and she's putting a lot of trust in you that you're not going to."

Sam has drawn open the curtain over his bed, and he gazes up into the bright green hills behind the house. Perched on the very edge of suburbia, defending the outermost urban perime-ter. The birch and cottonwoods wave to him like teasing soldiers, dare him to buck the social order, deny his birthright, join them in uncontrolled proliferation beyond the insidious grasp of the superego. But where does the wilderness truly end and civili-zation begin? Probably several townships in, if at all. "I know, Roger. It scares the hell out of me."

"Yeah, well." Roger clears his throat. "Sorry. I didn't call to lecture you. I'm just on my way to Mass, and then my family's eating lunch at my Grandma's, so I wanted to make sure you were still planning on seeing the play tonight with me and Mi-chele."

"Yeah," says Sam slowly. He feels on the desk for his glasses, slips them on. The trees snap into sharp focus and the pain in his head redoubles. "We're still planning on it."

"All right, we'll see you at six, then. Take it easy."

"Sure." Sam hangs up. He considers calling Donny back, but doesn't think he could play a decent game now. Instead, he wan-ders downstairs to the living room, still in his pajamas, and touches a few keys on the console piano in the corner opposite the fireplace.

"Sam," calls his mother from the kitchen, "I'm working night shift at the hospital again tonight, so I won't be home when you leave. Will you need anything to eat this evening before you go?"

"No, we're eating at the Seven Samurai, in the city." He sits down on the bench, caresses a dominant seventh. "Roger's idea."

"Well, one of these nights when I'm off I want you to invite those little friends of yours over for dinner, especially Kate. This kitchen's too big for just the two of us . . . Now why don't you come down and have some breakfast?"

"Okay, Mom." His left hand travels up and down the keyboard in an exotic progression, and his right furnishes a delicate obligato, but Sam can't tell whether the mode is major or minor.

III

SUNDAY EVENING

COLORS RANGING FROM BLOOD-RED THROUGH DANDELION-YEL-
low clear to new-denim-blue wash and bleed across the sky, the
way the pattern on the surface of a puddle of oil changes as
you move your head. Sam rings the doorbell, and the sound of
chimes echoes back to him from deep within the bowels of the
house, followed by a gabbling horde of children's voices, all eager
to be the first to scope out big sister's beau. A light breeze teas-
es his hair; he clamps a hand down over his bangs. The ornate
door swings open and Kate appears, face in shadow, holding off
her younger siblings. An alluring nimbus of kinky, backlit hair
dances around her head, down past her shoulders. "Hi, Sam," she
says stoically and moves onto the porch, tossing a quick goodbye
over her shoulder and trying to stem the tide of little brats.

Her mother surfaces suddenly in the midst of the fracas, an
older, slightly imperfect replica of her daughter, shooing the
children away from the door. "Have a nice evening, you two,"
she says, smiling up at Sam. "Don't forget there's school in the
morning."

"Take your time getting there," calls a rough voice from a nearby room, "but hurry back." It chuckles at its own cleverness.

"We always do, Mr. Fitz—" But the door has already shut, sealing the young ones inside. Sam turns toward the driveway, where Roger and his date wait in the idling white Saab, and Kate latches onto his arm. "I never knew what I was missing, being an only child," Sam comments dryly.

"Oh, that's nothing. You should see them when they're eating sugar." She fingers a small gold locket dangling at her throat.

Sam chuckles appreciatively. "So, how've you been?"

"Just wonderful." In the late-evening light, her lipstick matches the copper-colored spill of hair about her shoulders. He wonders idly what lipstick tastes like. "How about you?"

"Can't complain. Well, I guess I could, but it wouldn't do much good. Complaints can get wrapped up in a lot of red tape." Kate's laugh is soft and lilting. He pauses before opening the car door. "Besides, there's no reason to complain. I'm out on a lovely evening with an even lovelier girl. What more could I ask for?"

A kiss of color stains her cheeks, and her eyes linger on his for just a nonce before she ducks into the car and scoots across the back seat.

The afterimage of those eyes dances on his retinas for a long moment. Pale, pale blue—the color of arctic ice, just before melting . . . or better, the hue of the eastern sky a touch in front of sunrise. But deeper than the blue, there lies . . . something else. Something elusive, something unnameable. Yet Sam sees it, the way an old prospector sees the promise of gold in a bare stretch of rock. And what he sees may turn out to be as precious as that gold.

Shaking his head, he follows her into the car and locks the door.

DINNER IS SUPERB. SATED, BELLIES WARM WITH FRIED RICE AND Szechuan pork, their conversation turns introspective, contemplative, comfortable. The words flow with the lazy, unhurried surety of a wide, winding river. Roger and Michele discreetly refrain from intruding themselves: to Sam they look like a couple brought miraculously to life from the pages of *Vogue* or *Gentlemen's Quarterly*, out for a high-profile night on the town, yet he self-indulgently visualizes Kate and himself as the more perfect match—more relaxed, less constrained by stereotypical roles.

But as evening flows into night and the scene shifts from restaurant to playhouse, Sam's equanimity slowly erodes. By the second act, he has worked up the nerve to take her hand, but shortly thereafter becomes aware of the other couple's furtive petting in the adjacent seats. His own hand grows cold and clammy, a thing not fit for touching, only for being wrapped in newspaper and stuck in the freezer. At intermission he excuses himself curtly, pleading thirst and cramped legs.

He stalks up the aisle, wearing his thinly disguised scowl like a brand. The water fountain in the lobby spits all over his cheek; he wipes it brusquely away with a balled fist, and as he does so, a cool hand touches his shoulder. "Sam? Are you all right?"

He turns, Kate's hand sliding lightly down his arm to brush his knuckles. "Yeah, I'm fine," he says, forcing a smile. His eyes roam about the lobby—the politely disinterested patrons, the gold brocade dripping from the walls, the fragile chandeliers—dwelling anywhere but on hers. "I'm fine, really."

She takes his fist in her hands, gently soothing and smoothing it out flat. "Come on, Sam, you can talk to me. It's nothing I did, I hope."

"No, it's not you." Inertia works two ways: holding her hand was hard enough to do, but dropping it now is even harder. "It's a lot of things—mostly Roger right now, I guess."

"I know." She brushes an errant strand of hair back from his forehead. "I noticed it, too."

"It's just that—that he's trying to tell me how to act, how to play my cards, and it *that's* the example I have to follow . . ." Blood rushes to his cheeks. "I mean—"

The elusive spark resurfaces in Kate's eyes, and a slight smile graces her lips. Something about her has changed subtly, a minute shift in demeanor that Sam can only barely sense, in much the same way that you notice a persistent sound only after it has ceased. "I know what you mean," she says softly. The light hazing through her copper curls is painfully sweet. "I've often felt the same—"

Sam's eyes focus suddenly on two trim figures approaching from across the lobby. "Oh, my God," he breathes. "Kate, let's get back inside. The next act's probably about to start."

"Sam, what's the—"

"Yo, Sammy! Over here, kid!" The animated buzz of conversation in the lobby dies out for a second, like a drop-out on an audiotape, and the patrons study Corman with discreet disapproval. Muted black-on-black paisley sport coat, patterned shirt buttoned to the top with a gaudy brooch at the throat, and Nymph clad in slinky silk and clinging to his arm like a parasite—he's something alien to their experience. Kate draws close to Sam as they approach; Sam casts about nervously. The patrons reimmerse themselves in their own petty affairs.

"Good to see you, Sammy my man," Corman ebulliently greets him. His eyes trace Kate's lithe body, appreciatively. "I see you've taken our advice. Wise man." This with a subdued leer.

Kate looks a question at Sam, but he shrugs off both her gaze and Corman's comment. "You're the last person I expected to see here."

Corman grins his infectious grin, and his impeccably coiffed bangs wave in the slight draft like streamers of moss from a Spanish oak. "Yeah, well, it doesn't beat *Goldilocks and the Three Beavers* for entertainment, but someone had to be keeping tabs on you. No telling what kind of trouble you could get into on your own."

Nymph bares her teeth in a feral rictus, running her tongue lightly over the white enameled ridges.

The lights flash twice and dim. "Sorry, Corman, we've got to get back inside. Intermission's over."

Corman lays a hand on Sam's shoulder before they can leave and leans close to his ear. "Remember what I said about getting in trouble," he whispers conspiratorially. "You won't have to worry about it tonight, but I guarantee you will soon enough. Know what I mean?" He pulls back and winks.

"Good*bye*, Corman," says Sam stiffly and turns away with Kate—but not before Nymph can shoot the girl a look of pure contempt.

After that encounter, the theater seems dark, close, and oppressive. Even Kate's perplexed head on his shoulder, with her soft hair pillowed against his neck, can't dispel the gloom settling around him.

MOTHS ORBIT HELPLESSLY ABOUT THE DIRTY YELLOW PORCH light, casting wraithlike shadows across the mud-colored brick. The Saab idles impatiently in the driveway. Sam shivers in the chill.

"I had a great time tonight, Sam. I really did." She stands two steps higher on the porch than he, their fingertips barely touching. "Thanks a lot."

Sam pushes up his glasses, which have slid halfway down his nose. "I hope I didn't ruin the evening for you—back at the theater, I mean . . ."

"Don't be silly." She moves down a step, so her eyes are only a bit higher than his. "I'm getting to know the real Samuel Pauling, something few people have ever done, and I'm learning some amazing things." Sam looks away. "You're very rare, Sam. I don't know why they can't make them all like you."

"They broke the mold," he says simply.

Kate laughs and they draw together, easily. Sam's arms encircle her surprisingly slender waist; her fingernails caress his back, and he is acutely aware of her breasts pressing against his ribs. He pulls away gently, studies her face. Her pale, sparkling eyes dance unsurely across his features, locked with his own one moment, then fastened upon his lips, back up to his eyes, tracing along a cheek . . .

"Good night, Kate," he says unsteadily, suddenly realizing his eyes are moist. He blinks several times.

"I guess I'll see you at school, then. Or maybe at your chess meet." She takes a step backwards, up one stair, clasping the fingers of his hand.

"Yeah, I guess—I hope so." Their fingertips part. "Kate . . . thank you."

She flows gracefully up the steps and disappears into the house.

Sam slumps into his seat in the car, pinching the bridge of his nose, sits silently until Roger has dropped off Michele. "She said I was rare, Rog," he says into his hand.

With a sly smile, Roger backs out of Michele's driveway. "Well done."

"My mind is no longer functional. If that was a pun, your effort was wasted."

"But not yours." Roger adjusts the rearview mirror. "I'm predicting big things for you and Kate."

A long, slow breath leaks out of Sam's lungs. "What do you know about it?"

Roger chuckles at Sam's peevishness. "Listen, Sam, I've watched you two together all night. Now, I keep my eyes open, and I saw her acting ways with you she's *never* acted with anyone else."

"So?" Half defiant, half petulant.

"*So*, I think you and her are going to go a long way together."

"Yeah," Sam mutters. Exactly what he fears.

IV

MONDAY MORNING

SAM MAKES HIS WAY DELICATELY THROUGH THE KNOTS AND clusters of bodies that clog the school hallways like fatty build-up in an artery. His stomach still churns with the bus fumes just left behind. Jostled and tossed about like a leaf on the wind-ruffled surface of a pond, he drifts through the corridors in search of Corman, with whom he wants very much to have words. He spies Moose and Jen, arguing softly but heatedly over something in Moose's hand. He hurries by, eyes averted.

Near a wide intersection in the main hall, a flurry of motion explodes at the edge of his vision, and Jerry Thomkins, a small, bookish underclassman from the chess team, shoves past him, gasping a plea for help. Momentarily, the first of Jerry's pursuers flashes by, yelps, and plows into the tile with the force of a pile driver, taking a few bystanders down with him. His two companions lose momentum in the scattering, laughing crowd, and Jerry escapes.

Sam melts into the throng, favoring his right leg, trying to get away before he is spotted. He recognizes all three bullies from the party Saturday night, and they might guess it was he who had tripped their leader if they noticed him slinking away. One more thing to bring up with Corman.

Around the corner, he stops at the locker he shares with Roger, to unload some of his books. He keeps an eye on the milling crowd, alert for signs of trouble. A chattering clutch of girls passes nearby, and Sam spots Kate at its center, her eyes downcast. A goofy smile twists his lips, and he calls: "Morning, Kate."

Her girlfriends' eyes swivel toward him, like freely mounted laser emplacements. Then they burst into raucous giggling and sweep crimson-cheeked Kate away with them. Sam watches them disappear, rhythmic queasiness washing through his gut. She seemed so carefree last night, and now she looks miserable. Why did people have to be that way? More importantly, when would he wise up and stop bucking the social order?

The first bell clatters, and the halls begin to empty. On the way to first-period health, Sam runs into Corman, who is just seeing Nymph off with a kiss at the door to her classroom. "Hey, Corman, I've gotta talk to you."

"Atmosphere's all wrong now, Sammy," Corman says, sidling toward a nearby staircase. Nymph winks at Sam and enters her classroom. "Too many minds around, you know? You want to talk, meet me at my locker a half-hour after school." He vanishes down the stairs.

Confused, Sam walks slowly to health, beating the bell by just a few seconds. He slips into his desk, behind Donny Phu's, and rests his head on his forearms. During roll call, Donny turns slightly and whispers, "I got a problem, Sam."

Damn, not more already. "What kind?"

Donny opens the pocket of his down vest a little. "Lookit."

Sam peeks over the edge of the desk, and his eyes grow wide.

A bulging baggy of marijuana fills the pocket. "Cripes, where'd *that* come from?"

"I got here early this morning—to get on the computers, you know?—and good thing, too." Donny's eyes dart nervously behind his epicanthic folds; his tongue touches the bristly excuse for a mustache at the corners of his mouth. "Someone'd planted this shit in my locker—last Friday, I guess. I didn't know what to do with it, so I just stuffed it in my pocket. When I was walking away, one of those New Wavers—Scott Townshend—he's in this class—well, he showed up with the vice-principal, and the vice-principal opened my locker. I hid and they didn't see me, but I saw them, searching through all my books and stuff. Finally, the veep started lecturing this kid and went away—but Sam, I came *this* close this morning to getting framed for possession."

"Mr. Phu," says the teacher gruffly, "let's knock off the chatter, okay? There's important business going down here. First up this morning, class, I want to talk about suicide, and then we'll wrap up our unit on mental health from last week. Now, I have seven items I'm going to read to you, and I want you to write them down. They're the seven warning signs of a potential suicide, and you never know if they might show up on an exam . . ."

"What do I do with this grass, Sam?"

Donny's whiny voice is getting to Sam. "Keep it," he whispers. "We can use it later to frame Scott or something."

"Hell, Sam, I already got him back. I left a bunch of dirty messages in some girls' files on the computer system this morning, and I set 'em up so they were tagged with Scott's password. They should be logging on just about now and becoming very offended."

"So you've had your revenge. Keep the stuff for yourself. Throw a goddamn party. I don't care what you do with it." Sam puts his head down again, trying to tune out the world, but the grating voice of his teacher rasps in his ears like sandpaper:

". . . severely depressed one day, elated the next, and depressed again the day after, may be struggling with the desire to live and the even stronger desire to die. Number three is when a person starts to give away the things he or she loves. This may be a way of telling you—"

"Coach Renfro?" interrupts a crackling voice over the intercom. "The principal would like to see a Scott Townshend in his office right away if you can spare him."

"Yeah, okay. He's on his way. Well, go on, Townshend. You heard her. Get going."

Donny flashes Sam a smile of triumph.

NOON

Sam sees Kate again in the cafeteria, surrounded by her flotilla of girlfriends—girls with minds like the blisters on sheets of packing plastic. She looks morose, fingering her little locket, but her friends seem oblivious to this fact.

Roger spies the girls, too. "C'mon, Sam. Let's eat over there."

Sam dissuades him, politely.

VI

MONDAY AFTERNOON

"Just be patient for a minute, Sammy boy," says Corman with that infuriating insouciance of his, rearranging the books in his locker.

"But you can stop them," Sam says accusatorially. "You have the influence; they'll listen to you." He glares at Corman almost defiantly, the sounds of his anger echoing hollowly through the empty corridors of the school. The detritus of the lately departed mod lies on the floor like beached fish deposited by a passing wave: shredded candy wrappers; broken pencils; glossy photos cut from rock-and-roll rags, heartthrob tabloids, and motorcycle magazines; pages from old exams, heavy with blood-red checks and cross-outs. Soft, sad strains of Chopin waft through the hall incongruously, emanating from the humanities room where Mrs. Finch is working late.

Corman slams his locker shut; the wind generated scatters garbage past their feet. "I can't do anything," he says with his infectious grin. "Anything at all. If your hacker friends are get-

ting picked on, too bad. Complain to the principal, not to me."
He turns as if to leave.

Sam stays where he is. "Okay, then, here's another question.
How did you know I was going to be at the play last night? Who
told you?" His pause matches one of Chopin's: deathly silence.
"Was it Roger?"

Exasperation scribbled across his face, Corman turns back.
"Even your friend Roger's not *that* big a dick. God, Sam, c'mon.
Use your head. Where could I *possibly* found that out? You know,
don't you." The slow smile sneaks back. "You've seen me do it
before."

"Dammit, I'm not one of your drugged-out zombies! I don't
believe any of that bullshit!"

"You do," says Corman quietly. The Chopin prelude fills the
pause like air rushing into a vacuum. "That's why you're getting
so pissed off."

"*It is*—" Sam takes a deep breath. "It is not. You have no idea
why I'm . . . pissed off. You couldn't understand."

"Because you don't want everybody to think that Kate
Fitzhugh's a slut. Look, it doesn't matter what anyone else
thinks—and anyway, I took the liberty of asking Chet a little
question on your behalf."

Suspicious eyes squint. "Chet?"

"Don't look at me like that, man. Chet's what I call my board.
He says you're gonna score with Kate in a couple of days, and no
one's gonna call her a slut."

Sam walks away, feeling nauseous.

"Oh, come on. You want it."

"I do not." He has stopped, back turned, head down. He kicks
a wadded-up bathing beauty from *Sports Illustrated*.

"Everyone wants it, Sam. You know it."

Sam whirls in anger. "Why are you doing this to me?" His fists clench spasmodically.

Rather than answering, Corman removes his hand from his jacket pocket. He holds the wooden pointer from the ouija board. "This is called a planchette," he says, "Chet for short. Without one, any ouija board is useless. See, it interp—"

"I don't have time for this. I've got a match pretty soon."

Corman apparently doesn't hear him. "It interprets signals and energies from the world of the supernatural, makes it so we can understand them." He speaks quite seriously, without his usual levity. "See the little legs on the bottom? Sometimes you'll find a planchette with a pen or pencil there, instead of this third leg, for writing out messages on paper."

"You're crazy," says Sam. But he doesn't leave.

"Maybe so"—Corman pats the planchette fondly—"but at least I've got interesting company. Sam, with this little guy, I can do *anything*, find out anything I want to know. I can sit down with a newspaper, and Chet points to what stories I should read, what movies I'd enjoy. When I'm in a jam, he can help me pick the right answers on a test. Give him a calendar, and he can tell me which days to look out for. I've used him to help my old man out in the stock market, and he hasn't lost a penny yet. He helped me to find my perfect sex object, looking through last year's yearbook. Nymph gets off on power, man, raw power—and that's what I've got. Chet's done it all for me." He slowly turns the pointer over in his hands. "He's my best friend in the world."

"So why are you telling me this?"

"Watch this." Corman very gently sets the planchette on the floor at his feet, pointing at Sam, and takes a step back. Nothing happens for a moment, then it begins to quiver, like a hound suddenly catching wind of fox-scent. Drumming the warning tattoo of a pit viper, the little legs rattle on the floor, impatiently, nervously.

And it moves, an inch. Toward Sam.

The rattling continues for another pair of heartbeats, dies down to stillness like a tired animal settling in for the night. A tired little rat. Sam shakes his head, denying the occurrence to himself. But he is frightened.

"He wants you, man," says Corman, and is it just Sam's imagination, or does he hear in the statement a trace of jealousy, a dash of resentment? "He wants you so bad that he can transform potential spiritual energy into real kinetic energy, just so he can get closer to you. He wants you so bad, wants to be *shared* with you, that he won't do a damn thing for me when you're around—unless you're helping." His voice acquires an urgent, fevered edge. "Don't let him down, Sammy, don't. This is my best friend we're talking about here."

With a hand on his brow, Sam shakes his head. "Why? Why me?"

"Sam, look." Corman seems to be trying to recover his usual sense of jocularity. "If you still don't believe me, I'll prove it's true. Here"—he kneels, unravels and smooths out a crumpled sheet of paper from the floor—"this can be our board. Like I said, it doesn't matter what else we use; it's the planchette that's the important part." He takes a felt-tipped pen from his jacket pocket and quickly scrawls the alphabet in large, messy script. He sets the planchette on the makeshift ouija board. "Now ask a question, something from your childhood, something there's no possible way I could know. Do it."

Sam tries to think of something, but he can't tear his eyes away from the pointer sitting there on the paper like a little crab, waiting for some poor fishlike scrap of thought to dart too close . . .

Click!

Both heads turn at the sharp, hollow sound. A large, simian figure stands at the far end of the hallway, a portentous silhouette framed in a window blazing with the afternoon sun. Chopin's funereal melodies underscore its presence like well-crafted soundtrack. Its right arm is stiff, thrust forward, gripping something fiercely. "Lookee there," it says in a voice sharpened by drugs or fatigue or both. "Not exactly a bird-lady, are you."

Corman pushes himself to his feet, brandishing the planchette like a shield. "Moose, you're making a mistake. You're not supposed to *do* this, for Pete's sake. I told you it wouldn't work." His voice quavers, nonetheless.

Moose takes a step toward them; the pistol absorbs a ray of sunlight and flings it away evilly. "Yeah, and I'm supposed to do what a piece of wood tells me to, right? Fat fucking chance."

Sam backs up a little, eyeing the hall around the corner. Moose has got nothing against *him*. He could make a break for it . . .

"You're not talking sense." Little beads of sweat condense like dew on Corman's brow. "What's going to happen is already decided, and you trying to change it isn't gonna make a damn bit of difference."

"Sit still. I'm gonna prove you wrong." Moose's finger begins to tighten.

"Put down the goddamn *gun!*"

A door opens halfway down the hall, dowdy Mrs. Finch emerges from her classroom arcane. "*What,*" she demands imperiously, "is going on out—" Her face erupts in a spray of crimson, like a red rose coming violently to bloom. The shot echoes like receding thunder. Moose tosses down the gun and sprints off down a side-hall.

Corman chases after him, picks up the weapon, clamps it in both fists, and squeezes off two shots.

Numbly, Sam approaches the old lady. Her wide, ruined eyes stare up at him in mute supplication; the rest of her face is like pulverized meat. She spasms once, then goes limp. Her body looks as fragile and frail as that of a little bird, lying in a nest of crumpled paper, a broken, bleeding little . . . finch.

Sam's brain recoils, and he runs away in the opposite direction, Chopin wafting along in his wake.

THE ACHE BEHIND HIS EYES POUNDS MERCILESSLY, SCREAMING thoughts rattling inside his skull like dried seeds in a gourd. He grips the knob and leans wearily against the doorjamb before opening the stage door. He forces a weak smile for the benefit of the dozen-plus people on the stage. A smattering of games are already in progress, at tables scattered about like dropped jacks; Donny and Jerry, among others, are absorbed in their respective match-ups. The chess team's advisor frowns at his watch. "You're late, Sam. We were afraid you were going to no-show."

Sam glances out past the curtains at the wall-clock, a perfect round blemish on the chipped and cracked plaster of the auditorium. A red second hand sweeps across its face like a thin, bloody spike. A shudder thrills up his spine, out at his shoulders, and down his arms. The past hour he has spent bent over a clean porcelain bowl in the faculty men's room, trying but unable to rid his stomach of its contents gone sour. At last, he had mustered the fortitude to return to the scene—

—where Mrs. Finch's body was nowhere to be found.

The corridor of the shooting was as empty as a virgin's womb:

no trace of the body, not a spatter of blood. Even a good portion of the garbage had been cleared away. It was almost as if the incident had never occurred, as if the slate whereon Mrs. Finch's murder was chronicled had been wiped clean. But the erasure was incomplete; Sam's memory remains intact—if he can rely on it.

"Edling, will you please get your player seated so we can start this match? We haven't got all afternoon, you know." The teacher from Westmoreland High looks at Sam disdainfully.

Sam finds his way to his chair, opposite a serious-faced boy who looks just non-threatening enough to hint at the promise of a real challenge. The boy stretches a hand across the board. "I'm Mike Heywood."

Sam stares at the hand for a moment before remembering the etiquette. "Sam . . . Sam Pauling," he says, shaking Mike's hand weakly.

"I've heard of you, Sam. You're supposed to be pretty good. Good luck."

"Yeah . . . you, too."

As Mr. Edling reads the match rules, Sam glances out at the tiny audience. Roger sits with Kate in the fraying theater-like seats; Kate gives Sam a little wave. Sam grimaces back, wishing she and Roger would sit apart. A few other viewers are scattered about, friends and family of the other players, whose moves are detailed on a brace of overhead projectors. He sees no one else he knows.

The drone of Edling's voice fades out, and the man places a digital timer on the table. "We drew numbers before you got here, Sam. You open." He presses a button and the liquid-crystal numbers begin their race toward the three-minute limit.

Sam is White. And almost from the start he is losing. He

feels his ability to look ahead at the consequences of moves slipping away from him, like a sandcastle dissolving in the tide. His opponent probes his defenses delicately at first, and finds them wanting. Piece after piece falls to a steady Black onslaught; Sam finds himself more and more unable to defend his king. His second rook has just been taken when Corman enters the auditorium.

The soft creak of the door distracts him from the game and he looks up. Corman glances at the overhead projectors, grins at him, and makes the thumbs-up sign. Dried blood stains the digit. A sudden wave of nausea floods over Sam, and he lays his face in his hand, breathing deeply until he can look at the board again. But the pieces there blur and run together, swirling like oil stirred into a glass of water. It all turns gray, and Sam cannot tell his own pieces from his opponent's . . . can't tell the right from the wrong. Dammit, which piece is which? What the hell do I do?

If I just had Corman's pointer, he thinks suddenly. Then I could—

Shocked at himself, Sam breaks free of the thought, looks nervously around the stage and the auditorium, fearful the small audience can see right through him, that they know what just went through his mind. And then he hears a small voice call his name:

Sam. Help me, Sam.

It comes from the chessboard. Mrs. Finch's face gazes up plaintively from its gridded surface—from his queen's position. The ivory crown rest precariously on her iron-gray hair, and she looks frightened. He picks up her frail body, moves her ahead three squares, plunks her down next to a giant black steed astride which sits Corman, grinning idiotically. *Begone, foul knight!* she commands regally, brandishing her scepter at him. The black steed leaps mightily from the board, while Corman throws Sam a jaunty salute. Mrs. Finch is left standing alone on the ebony square.

A sudden roar comes from ahead of her and to the left, as an impossibly huge black pawn with Moose's face charges into her square, brandishing the ugly, gleaming pistol. A tongue of flame leaps from its barrel, and the queen falls to the ebony floor, her china-doll face cracking straight down the middle. Angry blood drips from the crack to stain her snow-white gown. As she fades from view, the two halves of her face stare helplessly at Sam, and he reaches to her.

But she is gone. His hand closes on the pawn, and he begins to squeeze—

Fingers touch his wrist. "That's *my* piece."

The observers from Westmoreland are murmuring, Sam realizes suddenly. His own friends and his advisor look at him in confusion, and he sees that Corman has gone quite pale. Sam studies the board, realizes what he has done. He took a Black knight with his queen—stupid move!—and left it vulnerable to attack from a pawn. A bloody *pawn*, for God's sake!

He releases the piece, knowing that move has cost him the match. "I concede," he says shortly and rushes from the stage.

"YOU KNOW, SAM," SHE SAYS SHYLY, "I'M GETTING A LITTLE TIRED of chasing you like this all the time."

Sam looks up from the dim interior of his locker, pushes his glasses up he bridge of his nose. He is kneeling, a few books in his hand. Kate has rounded the corner of the hall and stopped, about twenty feet away. The late afternoon sun beams through the trees outside the window, casts moving, dappled shadows over her body, and her features slip in and out of darkness with the timidity of a kitten. Sam's mouth trembles in parody of a smile, and he looks down again. "Yeah, well . . . I guess you need your exercise."

She chuckles softly and moves to him. He flinches a little as she brushes the hair back from his ear. "You know who you remind me of in those glasses?"

"Who?"

Her hand glides down to the back of his neck, which she massages with a touch as light as silk. "The Walrus."

He looks up blankly.

"You know, John Lennon?"

"Lennon got shot," he says hoarsely, and more viciously than he intended.

Her hand pauses. "You just threw away a match that meant a lot to you, Sam. Tell me what's wrong."

His eyes squeeze shut, lashes meshing like Velcro. "You don't want to know this time."

"Please. I . . . I've never known a guy with feelings as deep as yours, and I want . . . no, I don't *know* what I want." Her hand goes to her eyes. "I just see you like this, and it hurts that I can't do anything about it."

"Shit," he mutters, slamming his locker. He stalks away brusquely, without looking back.

"Sam," she pleads, but he doesn't stop. "What do I have to do?"

Nothing but his taut back, receding with the finality of the dot you get when you turn off you television.

"Do you want to see where I go when there's no one to talk to?"

He slows, shuffles to a stop.

"It's not far . . ."

A tiny turn to one side. A slight shrug.

To Sam, the lush green of the hills behind the school borders on ugly virulence, and every step deeper into the trees is like a descent into maelstrom—a colony of raging life that feeds on nothing but the dead matter of its forebears. Closing his eyes, he can see Mrs. Finch with finger-thick birch roots burrowing into her eye-sockets, out her nostrils, and back down her throat, sucking the fluids from her withered body, pulsing with barely contained vitality, finally emerging from—

But Kate's light yet insistent grip on his wrist keeps him moving, over hills and through gullies and down twisting streams, and as she leads, she talks. She talks of her childhood on a rapid succession of airbases, and of her friends, both at Buchanan and elsewhere, who were never more than just a group to belong to, and who could never accept the person she was, but only the person they wanted her to be. She talks of her parents: her father, gruff and rough and bluff, yet kind in his own peculiar way; and her mother, the only person who ever really understood her.

Eventually, she prods Sam into talking, too. He tells her about his friends and how they've always been persecuted, and he talks about his mother and how she does nothing but work herself to death at the hospital, and how his father left when he was little and he thought it was his own fault, and he speculates on why it happened, and why his mother never remarried.

But he doesn't mention the murder.

They have stopped, and the sun is disappearing, and before he knows what has happened he has kissed her for the very first time, and suddenly the forest doesn't seem like such a terrible place after all. Then she opens the little locket at her throat and shows him the picture of Jesus that her mother put there when she was little, to protect her and watch over her and keep her company when she had to be alone. Her eyes are sparkling again, as clean and alive as if a mountain freshet were gurgling and splashing along right behind her irises. He feels exposed before her gaze, stripped as bare as the death-white bones of a beached whale, bright and gleaming and defenseless and there for anyone to see. No secrets.

She laughs and flings her arms around him, the moment ends, and they trip lightly back to the parking lot. In her car, she kisses him again before dropping him off at his house and says maybe she loves him, and he gropes fruitlessly for a response until she is speeding off into the twilight and he is standing confused in his own driveway, the lightness in his mind suddenly vanished.

He can still feel the soft, warm touch of her lips on his own, and he buries his face in one hand, crying:

"My God, what have I done?"

VII

MONDAY NIGHT

HALF A MEATLOAF IN A TUPPERWARE DISH, A BOWL OF WILTING green salad, and a note from his mother saying she hoped his match went fine and could he get the dishes done before she came home from work? Sam crumples the note and backhands it into the wastebasket, then digs a carton of ice cream out of the freezer. His stomach needs soothing, not punishment.

He is turning a brown-splotched banana over in his free hand when the jangle of the telephone shatters the stillness of the kitchen, like a brick smashing through a window. He drops the ice cream and whirls, hands in the air, then exhales in relief. "Shit," he breathes, lifting the receiver. "Yeah, hello?"

"I think you're in deep trouble, man."

"Roger?" He scratches his neck with the end of the banana. "You scared me to death. I thought—"

"Shut up and listen, all right? I'm trying to save your ass." He breathes out sharply into the phone. "Some cops showed up at the school maybe five-ten minutes after you took off. Wouldn't let any of us leave. Someone apparently found a dead body in one of the johns."

Black thoughts descend over Sam's mind like a shroud. He had almost managed to convince himself that it had never happened, and now— "They're coming here, aren't they."

"To your house, Kate's house, Corman's—they're looking for anyone who might have been in the school this afternoon, who might have seen anything." Awkward silence. "Corman got you involved in all this, right?"

"Don't be silly. I know less than you do."

"Corman tried to follow Kate when you took off at the match, but I wouldn't let him. Then when he heard the sirens outside, he told me to warn you in case he couldn't get a hold of you, and then he snuck out."

"Well, now you've warned me. Catch you later."

"Sam, wait a—"

He starts to dial Corman's number almost before he has hung up on Roger. A series of distant clicks echoes back from the far ends of the phone line, and a busy signal sounds. He wipes tiny beads of sweat from his lip and redials, but the busy signal drones on with the steadiness of a homing beacon. He drops the receiver, sprints to the front door. His battered Impala, so hashed that he rarely drives it, starts with a cough, and he backs it recklessly into the street.

Sam doesn't know why he's fleeing. He tries to figure it out as he careens madly through the streets of the depressingly similar subdivisions. He tries to tell himself that there's nothing to worry about, that he's only a *witness* to murder, not an accessory—but a confused jumble of images assaults him along the way, destroys his chain of reason. His fingers on the planchette that condemned a boy to commit murder—rolling hills forested with giant black chessmen—an old lady's withered arms wrapped lovingly around his body—his own hand curled around the butt of a wicked pistol—a young woman lying faceless on a tile floor, copper hair soaked to the roots in blood and studded with little bits of cheesy gray-bluish matter—

He slams on the brakes suddenly, brings the car skidding to a halt. That's not how it happened, none of it! he rages. He beats on the steering wheel with his fists until the images go away, then leans back, breathing heavily. When he thinks he has himself under control, he looks around to see where he is.

His car is slewed around at the edge of the street, half in and half out of Corman Kendricksen's driveway. He pulls the car out and parks it a little more neatly at the curb, then jumps out in a rush. The house is dark but for the eerie television-glow flickering in the front window. A gibbous moon hangs just above the lip of the flat roof. It follows Sam like a giant half-lidded eye as he races up to the door. His knock meshes gracefully with the faint sounds of a war movie inside.

The door squeaks open. An unshaven, potbellied man in a T-shirt peers through the screen. "Yeah, what do you want?"

"I wanna see Corman."

"Sorry, kid. Corman's busy. He ain't seein' nobody." The door begins to close.

"Wait!" Sam says, putting a hand to the screen. "Tell him Sam's here."

The man reappears. "Sam?" He unlocks the screen door and holds it open, casting furtive glances in every direction. "Corman said to let you in if you showed up. Wait jus' a minute and I'll get 'im for you."

Sam paces the living room while the man goes to the bottom of the staircase. "Corman, your man's here. Corman?" Tortilla chips and empty beer cans litter the rug like fallout from the video war. Sam can't tell if the litter is fresh or if it's a remnant of Saturday night's party. The man slouches back to his armchair and settles down. "He'll be down in jus' a second. He wants you should wait here."

Sam's pacing continues, and he eyes Corman's father with the dirty T-shirt. "So how's the stock market?" he finally asks.

The man lifts an eyebrow. "Lost a shitload today."

"No kidding?" Sam stops his pacing, puzzled.

"Yeah. Gosh-damnedest thing, too. I don't mind tellin' you this 'cause it seems like Corman trusts you." He shifts in his chair, scratches his belly, never looking away from the comic-book violence playing out on the wide screen. "I thought I had myself a safe little investment, steady growth, a little profit and all. The this morning—*boom!*—it goes right through the floor, you know? I figgered it'd happen sooner or later, but I wasn't expectin' nothin' like this. Hell, it'd been six months since I'd even lost a coupla bucks. I guess Corman's . . . financial advisor ain't perfect, huh?"

Sam's eyebrows rise. "Corman's financial advisor? Have you ever met this . . . advisor of his?"

"Naw. Corm jus' brings me the guy's predictions on a little slip of paper. I never actually . . . Say." Kendricksen finally looks away from the television. "You're not . . . ?" He shrugs lamely, as if that completes the question.

Sam falters under the man's gaze. "No, I'm not the one." He shakes his head slowly, eyes on the filthy rug. "Not me."

A clatter of feet caroms down the staircase. "C'mon, Sam. Follow me." Corman doesn't pause for a moment in his rush through the room. "I don't know when we'll be back in, Dad. Hopefully before too long. Come *on*, Sam." The final words echo in from the kitchen.

"No problem," calls the elder Kendricksen. More shells burst, and he is lost once more in video-rapture.

Corman has already stormed through the back door by the time Sam enters the kitchen. It gapes like a mouth into void, the moonlight beyond painting the ash trees and the chain-link fence a pale silver—the color of old statuary. Corman kneels on the damp, metallic-seeming grass, takes the ouija board from under his arm and sets it before him. He looks up as Sam approaches. "Dammit, close the back door," he says, as if Sam should have done it without being told. He takes his planchette from the pocket of his jacket, makes a few passes with it over the board. "Not strong enough." He moves closer to the back fence and tries again. "Interference. We should have had a wooden fence." Scooping up his arcane hardware, he scoots closer to the house. "Here it's about as good as we're going to get. Kneel down, Sammy."

Sam takes a position across the board from Corman. "What's the problem?"

"I tried to do this in the house, but the goddamn TV was generating too much static. It's pretty bad close to the fence, too, and out here we're getting screwed up by everyone's satellite dishes and shit. Right here's our clearest spot short of going up into the hills." Corman's face resembles a cold, stone mask in the moonlight.

"There wasn't any trouble with interference before."

"Last time we played with Chet, there were a dozen people standing around strengthening reception." He eyes Sam disdainfully. "Now there's just two of us. Gimme your fingers."

"Can—can I ask it something?"

"*Him*, stupid. About what?"

Sam flinches at the violence in Corman's tone. "It's about Kate and me, and—"

"You already know the answer to that question. I don't have

time to—"

"I don't know *anything* all of a sudden! I came here because I need help to figure it all out again."

"You've got a lot to learn," says Corman through clenched and silvered teeth. "You came here because Chet damn well *wanted* you here."

"Why?" Sam leaps to his feet and thrusts a trembling finger at the pointer. "Why the hell does it want *me?*"

Corman's lips frame an angry retort, but no sound comes out. "I don't know," he confesses at length. "Something important's gonna happen here tonight." As his voice falls to a whisper, the jealousy in it is palpable. "And whatever it is, it revolves around *you.*"

Sam says nothing, just glares steadily down at Corman with pupils the size of rifle bores.

Corman looks away. "Do you realize what you did to me today? At your damn chess meet?"

"You lost a bet. Tough shit. Your little toy there *told* you I was going to concede. You should've listened to it."

"I know, I *know.*" Corman wipes his face with the back of his hand. "I thought— Well, screw what I thought. You know what I thought." He turns the pointer over in his hands, scratches its underside like you'd scratch the belly of a dog. "The damn thing tricked me."

"It just answered your question."

With an air of defeat, Corman lays the planchette down on the board and leans way back. "You still don't know who the bet was with, do you."

Sam shakes his head no.

"Well, it was with Chet. We were talking one day, and he offered me this wager. We bet on your chess match, and whoever won was supposed to grant the other one a wish. It sounded like fun . . ."

"But then you lost."

"Thanks to you."

Sam doesn't rise to the bait. "And you had to grant it a wish."

Corman nods.

"So what was the wish?"

Corman looks up slowly, and something glistens in the corner of his eye. "He wants me to give him to you."

Sam's first impulse is to turn it down; he can see how hurt Corman feels. But when he speaks, a deeper cruel impulse surfaces. "So what the hell am I supposed to do with it?" he says viciously.

"Who ever said I was going to give it to you, huh?" retorts Corman, suddenly embittered.

Sam sits down; the wetness of the grass seeps through the seat of his jeans. "From what I've seen in the past few days," he says, his voice gentle, "I doubt you can keep it from doing what it wants."

"I know." Corman sighs, then stands and paces restlessly away from the board. "I should never have taken the damn bet in the first place." He pounds his open palm with his fist. "I thought it was just a stupid game. I should have known."

Sam forms a church-and-steeple of his fingers, rests his chin on the outstretched porch of thumbs, strokes his nose with the spire of forefingers. He chooses his words carefully. "Corman . . . why *am* I here, do you think? Just to take your planchette away from you? Or is it something more than that?"

The nervous pacing stops, and Corman stands facing away from Sam for a few moments, head down. Then resolutely he turns, his face once more an icon of stone. "Well, why don't we ask?"

Corman sits, and they reposition their fingers on the pointer. He nods curtly to Sam, indicating that he should ask the question. Sam concentrates momentarily, then says simply: "Why are we here?"

W . . . A . . . T . . . E . . .

"That's all I've been getting all night," Corman says, with more than a trace of malicious pleasure. "All it says is wait wait wait. Something's gonna happen. Just wait." He hawks and spits through the chain-link fence. "I'm sick to death of waiting." A thrust of his legs, and Corman is on his feet, stalking toward the corner of the house.

Sam's hand still rests on the planchette. It moves suddenly, and Sam's eyes snap wide open. "Corman, it's saying something else . . . s . . . T . . . A . . . Y . . . Stay. It wants you to stay."

Corman whirls violently. "Tell him up yours! If he thinks he can just dump me like I'm some kinda cheap whore than he damn well can't expect me to jump when he says jump!" He kicks open the gate to he driveway and marches away defiantly, as if daring anyone to stop him.

As the metallic echo dies away, a car pulls into the driveway, spotlighting Corman like a wild animal in its headlights. He freezes, then bolts back toward Sam. "It's the police!" he gasps, breaking stride only momentarily to snatch the planchette out from under Sam's hand. "Let's blaze!"

Car doors slam, shoes clatter on concrete, and Sam hears the same hollow click he first heard in the corridor at school. "Hold it right there!" shouts an authoritative voice.

Sam slowly raises his hands, seeing in his mind once more an erupting mushroom of blood, an old lady's ruined face. Corman, halfway over the back fence, drops to the ground and stands with his precious pointer tucked under one arm. "What seems to be the problem?" he says sweetly.

A man in a rumpled trench coat passes through the gate, wielding a large pistol. "Detective Edges, Lincolnsboro Police. Are you Corman Kendricksen?"

"Yes, and this is Sammy Pauling, my partner in crime." His smile twitches.

"That's fortunate." Edges holsters his weapon, but leaves the flap unsnapped. "We have some questions we'd like to ask both of you."

Sam's arms drop to his side, and he swallows a big lump of phlegm. "What kind of questions?"

"Agnes Finch, a teacher at Buchanan High School, was murdered there this afternoon between the hours of three and four o'clock. Witnesses can place the both of you near the scene of the crime during that time frame. We'd like to know if you may have . . . *seen* anything unusual."

Sam looks helplessly at Corman, who just shrugs.

A second detective joins the first. "Back-ups are on the way," he says, then takes in the scenario. "Want 'em canceled?"

Edges reflects for a moment. "No, we may still need them. That one over there"—he motions with his hand at Corman—"that one seems a little antsy. I think he knows something he doesn't want to tell anyone."

"How about this other one?"

"Yeah," drawls Edges, sizing up Sam, "what *about* this one?"

The tip of Sam's tongue moistens his lips as he fights the urge to look to Corman for help—a cue, a clue, what to do. The detective's eyes scrutinize him like those of a predator.

"Okay, boys," says the man at last, "if you're not willing to cooperate with us, we'll be forced to arrest you both on suspicion of murder." He hitches up his slacks, which tend to ride down under the outcrop of his potbelly. "And it's only fair to warn you that we have the murder weapon and we have fingerprints, both from it and from the blood on the victim's body. Once you've been processed, we'll know for sure whether or not either of you were involved."

"You're shitting us, man," Corman says, his attempt at nonchalance failing miserably. "You can't arrest us on that kind of suspicion."

"Maybe not," concedes the cop, "but if we don't get any cooperation tonight, we can sure as hell have a couple of arrest warrants for you two by tomorrow morning."

"Corman killed her," Sam says suddenly. "I saw it. You'll find his prints on the gun."

"You lying bastard," Corman hisses. His free hand trembles, and the other grips the planchette fiercely enough to turn the knuckles as white as exposed bone. "I did no such thing."

"Only it wasn't in the restroom." Sam looks at no one as he speaks. "It was in the hall. He dragged her body into the john after she was dead."

The loud rattle of metal on metal, chain links being shaken and stressed.

"Hey, stop!" The younger detective bolts to the fence, gun drawn, and hauls Corman down to the ground. The wooden pointer pops out of Corman's grasp. The man straddles him, pulling out a pair of handcuffs. "Just where did you think you were going?"

"Read him his rights, Benson," says Edges, just a few paces behind. "This should be enough to hold him on until we can get a match on the prints." He turns to Sam, who stands with his back turned, head down. "Your story jibes with the evidence we've gathered so far. Are you willing to come down to the station and sign a statement?"

Corman screams as Benson struggles to cuff his wrists. He screams accusations at Sam, filthy accusations, threats, curses. They fall about Sam's shoulders like a rain of physical blows—senseless violence, intolerable abuse. His vision is tinged with red. "Yes, I'll come," he says spiritlessly.

Edges nods. "Good boy. We'll let you ride with the back-ups when they get here. You won't have to go in the same car as your . . . your friend there."

Sam turns to look at Corman. Benson is hauling him to his feet, and his arms strain desperately toward the planchette, which lies legs-up on the grass like a dead beetle. "Dammit I gotta have that!" he screams. "What the fuck are you trying to do? Gimme my—"

"For God's sake, son, settle down," Edges says, moving to help his partner. "Detective Benson killed a man last week for resisting arrest, and he was better-looking than you."

"Mother—"

Sam picks up the ouija board, takes a few more steps, retrieves the planchette.

Corman's struggles cease momentarily. "Bring me my things, will you, Sammy, please? Please, Sam?"

"These are mine," Sam says. A river of ice flows through his voice.

The banshee-wails of approaching squad cars fill the air as Benson and Edges drag their prisoner down the driveway. Mr. Kendricksen emerges from the front door clearly distraught, into a yard awash with the violence of red and blue revolving lights, and Sam takes advantage of the confusion to sneak out to his car and secret the ouija board and planchette in the trunk.

VIII

MIDNIGHT

A BLUE HONDA PRELUDE, NOSING ITS WAY BLINDLY THROUGH the maze of suburbia. Inside the car, a discussion.

"Sam, you don't know how embarrassing it is to have to leave work early to pick you up from the police station." Fleet patches of light from the passing streetlamps transform Mrs. Pauling's face into a grinning skull, sliding alternately from life to shiny death and back again.

"I witnessed a *murder*—I couldn't *help* it." Sam grinds his teeth, stares moodily out the window. "You make it sound like it was all my own damn fault."

"Don't you use that language with me, young man, and you'd damn well better believe it *was* your own fault. If you hadn't been running around with that Kendricksen boy, none of this would have happened."

"You mean *I* wouldn't have been involved. Well, if I hadn't been there when I was, Corman might have gotten away clean. You'd rather have a murderer running around free? Did you ever think of that?"

"I never liked him, never at all." Her mouth is set in a rigid line that not even the gentle dashboard lights can soften.

"Turn left up here. That's where I parked the car."

"Roger would never have gotten you into this kind of trouble," his mother says abruptly.

"No, if it was up to Roger, he'd be getting me into another kind of trouble altogeth— Dammit, Mom, I said turn *left*."

She stomps heavily on the brakes, throwing Sam into the un-yielding embrace of his inertial seat belt. "I'm *sorry*, Sam," she cries angrily. "It's just that I've never had a—a violent crime strike so close to my family, and I don't like it one bit." Reck-lessly she backs into the intersection, spins the wheel hard to the left, accelerates, and comes juddering to halt behind Sam's beat-up Impala. Her hands flutter helplessly, her eyes overflow with tears. "Now would you just get off my back?"

"Sure." Sam pushes his way out of the car, its finish dull as old gunmetal in the darkness. A bank of inky clouds has blotted out the moon. "Anything you want." And he slams the door violent-ly behind him.

WITH HIS SILENTLY FUMING MOTHER AT LAST ASLEEP IN HER own room, Sam pulls all the drapes, dims the lights, and seats himself atop the mound of pillows hastily arranged on his bed. The ouija board sits in his lap, his fingers touched lightly to the surface of the planchette. "I have only one question," he says wearily, all his anger spent, guilt seeping in to replace it, "and once you've answered it, I'm going to bed."

Chet waits patiently.

"What do you want me for?"

A shiver like a tiny jolt of electricity flows through his fingers,

and the planchette frames its answer: C . . . U . . . M . . . P . . .
A . . . N . . . I . . . E . . .

"C'mon, be serious."

T . . . O . . . C . . . K . . . T . . . O . . . M . . . E . . .

Sam blows out his breath. "I *am* talking to you. You gonna
answer my question or not?"

C . . . A . . . N . . . T . . .

"Oh, yeah? Why not?"

N . . . O . . . W . . . U . . . R . . . D . . . S . . .

"No words? Shit." Sam slumps against the wall, forehead
gleaming in the yellow light with a thin veneer of sweat. His
stomach growls emptily and he sways a little, like a man aboard
ship for the first time. It doesn't have the words to answer my
question. Great.

T . . . O . . . C . . . K . . . G . . . I . . . V . . . E . . . M . . . E . . .
W . . . U . . . R . . . D . . . S . . .

"Didn't Corman . . . give you words? Or is that why you're
such a lousy speller?"

R . . . I . . . T . . . E . . . O . . . N . . .

Feeling rather foolish, Sam proceeds to "give wurds" to the
eager planchette. Trivia dribbles from his mouth, and Chet responds in kind—but as the exchange continues, the thing's vo-
cabulary, spelling, and grammar steadily improve. By one in the
morning, it is as well-spoken as any professional orator, and its
hypnotic power is no less subtle.

THATS ENOUGH FOR NOW THANKS SAM, it spells out.

Fatigued, Sam rubs his eyes. "Lord. What time is it?"

A HAIR PAST I . . . YOU READY FOR SOME SERIOUS SHIT? . . .

"I'm ready for some serious sleep. Good night."

WAIT . . . I HAVE ENOUGH WORDS TO ANSWER YOUR QUESTION
NOW . . .

"It can wait until morning."

IT IS MORNING DUMMKOPF . . . LISTEN . . . YOU HAVE A GOAL
AND I HAVE A GOAL . . . THE MEANS TO ACHIEVE EACH END JUST
HAPPEN TO COINCIDE . . .

"They just *happen* to, huh? Sorry, but I don't believe in that
kind of coincidence."

MAYBE THATS SO BUT YOU SHOULD STILL LISTEN FOR A MIN-
UTE BEFORE YOU DISMISS MY PLAN OUT OF HAND . . .

Sam blinks his tired eyelids open. "Okay, what's your plan?"

IT ENTAILS A CHANCE FOR YOU TO MAKE SURE THE CONFLICT
BETWEEN YOUR FRIENDS AND CORMANS ENDS BEFORE ANYONE
GETS SERIOUSLY HURT . . . INTERESTED? . . .

Something taps against the window, but Sam dismisses it as an
insect or a branch in the wind. "Maybe. What do I have to do?"

THERE ARE CERTAIN PEOPLE WHO MAY INTERFERE WITH THE
COMPLETION OF OUR PLAN . . . I SET UP APPROPRIATE SITUA-
TIONS AND YOU NEUTRALIZE THESE PEOPLE . . .

"Neutralize?" The desk lamp flickers like a candle guttering in
the wind, and Sam shivers as if a cold breeze has sliced through
his body. The tapping sounds again. "What the hell does that
mean?"

NOT TO KILL . . . JUST NEUTRALIZE . . . LIKE YOU DID TO
CORMAN TONIGHT . . . HE WAS A MAJOR THORN IN BOTH OUR
SIDES . . .

A finger of guilt stabs Sam through the gut. "I *lied* tonight.
You want me to do that again?"

YOU DIDNT LIE . . . NOT THAT HE ACTUALLY PULLED THE
TRIGGER BUT THATS BESIDE THE POINT . . . HE WAS TOTALLY
SELF CENTERED AND COULDNT UNDERSTAND THE NECESSITY
OF USING ME FOR OTHER THAN PERSONAL GAIN . . . HE HAD TO
GO . . .

A small shower of pebbles bounces harmlessly off Sam's window. "Who's out there?" he whispers, suddenly frightened.

ITS OK . . . GO SEE . . .

Clutching the planchette in his hand, Sam slips off the bed and pads over to the window. He shades his eyes against the dull glow of the desk lamp and surveys the backyard. Something, a dark figure, crouches in the bushes beneath the window, gathering up tiny rocks from the ground. The figure looks up, arm cocked to toss the little stones against his window. Sam sucks in his breath. The face is no more than a pale smear against the dark night, but it is unmistakably Nymph's.

He slides open the window and hisses viciously through the screen: "What the hell are you doing here?"

"Come out and play, Sammy?" she singsongs.

"Go away!"

Nymph assumes a pouting stance, pleading at him with her big black eyes and outthrust lower lip and giving him a wonderful view down her black lace blouse. "Come on, Sam. I need to see you."

"You can see me from there," he says, tongue thick in his mouth. But he steps back from the window, sets the planchette back on the ouija board. "What do I do, Chet?" he asks.

GO . . . SHE MAY HAVE SOMETHING USEFUL TO SHOW YOU . . .

Uncertainly, he returns to the window. "I'll be down in a second." He rummages in his closet for his best denim jacket, the closest thing to vogue he owns, then shrugs into it as he tiptoes out of his bedroom and down the creaky stairs. Nymph waits just outside the back door, her white makeup glowing in the night like a full moon. She is on him almost before he has the door shuts, hands snaking beneath his jacket and roughly caressing his back. "What the hell—" he manages to say, turning away from the door and sliding completely into Nymph's embrace. Before he knows what's happening, her mouth has sealed off his protest.

He pushes at her shoulders, but she is strong and determined. Pressed against her, he can feel every contour of her lithe body, the modest swell of her breasts, the smooth plateau of belly, the sweet, mysterious hollow of her thighs. He tries to force her away, to speak, but, when his mouth opens, in darts her uninvited tongue. Sam nearly gags. Her lips work as furiously as a carnivore's, and he feels his resistance being devoured.

The rhythm of the hands on his back and the body undulating against him are strangely hypnotizing, and when she begins to pull away gently, he follows her like an obedient child. She leads him to the small stand of cottonwoods in the far corner of the yard—moon-silvered trees that look like the puffy ends of giant buried cotton swabs—pulls him down to the grass, and reaches for the buckle of his belt. Her mouth fastens back onto his. The lace blouse has somehow fallen away, and, with the scent of girl and earth heavy in his lungs, Sam discovers the marvel of her warmth in the cold night.

IX

TUESDAY MORNING

TWO GREAT SHUDDERING COUGHS, AND SUDDENLY HE IS DROWN-
ing in phlegm. He sits bolt upright, fighting back the panic that
rises in his throat. Two more coughs and the offending matter
slides into his mouth like warm butter. He swallows it back with
a wince. His throat is as sore as if it had been scoured with sandpaper.

He sinks slowly back to the pillows and pries open his sleep-
gummed eyes. Late-morning sun streams through his curtains,
full of glittering dustmotes. Sam coughs again. His head hurts.
His nose is stuffed so badly he can only breathe through his
mouth. He shivers with chills. The cheerful sunbeam seems to
mock his illness.

He has no conscious memory of leaving the stand of cottonwoods.

His clock says eleven-thirty. He sits up again, swinging his
legs over the side of the bed and reaching for his robe. A grimace
seizes his face like rictus; his back feels like hell and his hips are in
agony. He stands, slowly and stiffly, and shuffles to the bathroom.

A note awaits him there, taped to the mirror. It drifts maddeningly in and out of focus. He reads it once perfunctorily, trying to control the swimming letters, then reads it again. It is from his mother, saying how he was running a fever and coughing and that she thought he should stay in bed and apologizing for yelling at him but murder is such an ugly business and telling him she was working early to cover for a friend who had to take the day off and informing him that Kate had been worried and called soon after school started because he hadn't been there and asking him to maybe finish the meatloaf for lunch.

Sam shakes his head; the words run together like drops of water streaming from a tap. Kate's name seizes his attention, and he stops trying to make sense of the note. He tries to picture her face in his mind, but finds he can't. He can see portions, one at a time—the coppery spill of her hair, replaced by her silk-smooth skin, followed by the piercing gaze of her pale blue eyes—but his mind seems incapable of assembling the parts into a meaningful whole. And when it finally does, the result is not Kate at all, but a grotesque parody: a doll with a patchwork face and a heaving, nubile body.

His stomach boils up suddenly, and he drops to his knees beside the clean white porcelain toilet bowl. When he retches, it is nothing but a small dribble of bile that scorches his mouth and throat. His stomach heaves like an empty pump, hurting him. He leans his head on the cool rim of the bowl, eyes squeezed shut. His breathing is ragged; when he finally brings it under control, he stands with weak knees and rinses his mouth and face. "What the hell do I do now?" he says to the bleary-eyed Sam in the mirror. Then he staggers back to his bedroom.

The ouija board is hidden beneath the covers at the foot of

his bed. He retrieves it and sits cross-legged on the disordered mound of pillows. "What the hell do I do now?" he asks again, no longer rhetorically.

NOT FEELING GUILTY ABOUT LAST NIGHT ARE YOU SAM? . . .

"*Yes*, dammit, I—" He stops, abruptly conscious of the absurdity of screaming at a block of wood. "I feel guilty."

BUT WHY? . . .

"Because I . . . No, forget it. You wouldn't understand."

HOW MUCH DO YOU WANT TO BET? . . . SORRY BAD JOKE . . . BUT I KNOW WHAT YOURE THINKING AND ITS SOMETHING YOURE GOING TO HAVE TO LEARN TO SAY EVENTUALLY . . . SO SAY IT . . .

"All right, already. It's because . . . because I . . ." Sam never expected it to be such a difficult thing to say, even to someone uninvolved. It sounded so *easy* when *she* said it. "It's because I think maybe I'm in love with Kate."

THERE THAT WASNT SO HARD . . . NOW TELL ME WHAT YOU INTEND TO DO ABOUT IT . . .

"I don't *know*. I don't know if I can look her in the eye after . . . after the disgusting things I did with that disgusting thing."

DON'T BE SO HARSH . . . IM SURE NYMPH HAS FEELINGS TOO . . .

"The second time we did it, she made me take her by *force*, she made me brutalize her. I don't even want to *think* about what happened the third time. The girl's a goddamn *masochist!*"

SO FORGET HER . . . CHALK IT UP TO EXPERIENCE . . . CONSIDER IT PRACTICE FOR THE REAL THING . . .

"The *real* thing? Let me tell you, that was pretty *real* last night. I don't think I could get any realer than that if I tried."

LAST NIGHT WASNT REAL . . . YOUR HEART WASNT IN IT JUST YOUR BODY . . . IT WAS AN AUTONOMIC PHYSICAL PROCESS . . . WITH KATE IT WILL BE REAL . . .

"Look, this is pointless. I couldn't even *think* about being with Kate like that, not after what I did."

YOUVE GOT TO MAKE IT RIGHT WITH YOURSELF SOMEHOW . . . BUY HER SOMETHING NICE . . . SHOW YOURSELF YOU STILL CARE ABOUT HER . . .

"Oh, right. You want me to buy her love."

HOW CAN YOU BUY SOMETHING YOU ALREADY HAVE? . . . TRUST ME . . . DO THIS AND YOULL FEEL MUCH BETTER . . . I HAVENT STEERED YOU WRONG YET HAVE I? . . .

"Okay, okay, I'll do it. Just quit bugging me about it."

TUESDAY AFTERNOON

THE CITY MALL IS BIG—FAR TOO BIG FOR SAM'S TASTES. FOUR concourses stretch away from him like the points of a compass, each sprinkled with a handful of early-afternoon shoppers, mostly truant wanna-bees, unemployed trendies, women dressed and coiffed like secretaries, and a businessman or two. Four hanging Lucite signs list the stores in each concourse. A gang of punk rockers loiters insolently near the mouth of the west concourse, harassing the passing wannabes. Sam sniffles and turns to the east. Spiked hair makes him very nervous.

He passes a computer shop with barely a backward glance. Normally he would have spent an hour there, drooling over the latest software or graphics printer, but today computers seem simple and pedestrian compared to the companionship of an intelligent ouija board.

Sam ducks into the first novelty shop he sees, feeling a little silly and out of place. A small stuffed cartoon penguin catches his eye, between the teddy bears and the other huggable critters. The penguin wears a stupid grin on its oversized beak and holds a heart-shaped satin cushion behind its back. Awkward and insipid. Perfect.

As Sam is paying for the little toy, cool fingers touch the back of his neck and trace a little design. He turns. "Nymph!" he says in surprise, dropping back a step. The warmth in his voice shocks him.

"Fancy meeting you here," she says in return, slipping her arm through his. "I didn't have you figured for a sluffer."

"I . . . couldn't get up this morning," he says, fumbling for the right words. His pulse begins to throb in his temple. "And I wouldn't have been able to concentrate at school, anyway, not after, ah . . . not after what happened last night." As soon as it's out, he feels like kicking himself.

She glances at him appraisingly, with a touch of a smile on her lips. Her leopard-skin stirrup pants, bulky leather-and-denim jacket, and white lace choker somehow don't seem right next to his pinstriped oxford shirt and slightly faded 501's. Or perhaps it's the other way around. "I know what you mean," she says. "I was so sore this morning I could hardly stand up."

"That's not what I meant," he says hurriedly, accepting his change from the stone-faced cashier.

Nymph laughs. "C'mon, Sam, let's bum around for a while."

"I hate the mall. I don't like to stay any longer than I have to."

"Malls are a blast. You just have to be a little creative." She tugs him out of the store, and he clutches the little penguin close to his side.

OVER THE NEXT THREE HOURS, THEIR LITTLE UNIT OF TWO gradually snowballs to more than two dozen, hipsters every one, all buzzing with the news of Corman's arrest. They stride the concourses boisterously, play silly games on the escalators, improvise comedy routines, and generally intimidate the hell out of the ordinary law-abiding mall patrons. As promised, Sam is having the time of his life—for the first time *really* included in a marginally socially acceptable clique.

And amazingly, he is coming to truly *like* Nymph. Where he once thought of her as nothing more than a dim-witted, mute sex-kitten, she is now proving herself to be a witty, intelligent, and charismatically outspoken sex-kitten—and a lot of fun, besides. Sam feels an inordinate pride at parading around with her on his arm for everyone to see.

When its number approaches thirty—including an outrider group consisting of the same punkers Sam avoided earlier— Nymph calls the procession to a halt and, in tones of solemn authority, declares Samuel E. Pauling the successor to Corman the Tyrant as Chairman of the Board. A wild cheer sails forth, causing the more tremulous shoppers to cringe. Hands reach out to slip him some skin, slap him on the back, or tousle his hair. Then a rhythmic chant begins to rise, as compelling as the tattoo of African drums: "Speech, speech, speech . . ." His polite declination is shouted down enthusiastically; flustered, he waves the gathering down to near-silence.

"Uh, yeah, thanks," he stammers, "thanks a lot. This . . . means a whole lot. I, ah, hate to speak and run, but frankly, I've gotta pee so bad I'm seeing yellow. I move we hit the john, then reconvene this roadshow in ten. How 'bout it?"

More cheers—more scurrying shoppers—and the party migrates into the restrooms. Washing up in the crowded room after taking care of business, with his stuffed penguin sitting and grinning stupidly on the counter, Sam spies a familiar face in the mirror, back near the stalls. A face from Saturday, from school, a face once unfriendly—

"I got the shit back," the boy announces, producing a bulging bag of marijuana from his jacket pocket. "Who's got the zig-zags?"

A rabble of takers surrounds him as Sam turns from the sink, shaking the water from his hands. "You got that back from where, Scott?" he asks.

Scott shrugs. "This gook kid ripped it off from me, so me and some other guys kicked his ass and got it—"

Sam grabs him by the lapels and slams him hard into the wall. "You tried to frame that kid for possession, asshole," he growls, shaking the boy for emphasis. "He spoils your plan, makes off with the pot, and so you and your buddies beat him up. Real manly, real sportsmanlike. Well, I'm not going to have any of it." With his left forearm pressed against Scott's throat and collarbone, Sam relieves him of the baggy and tosses it into an unflushed toilet. No one says a word or makes a move to rescue it.

Sam releases the boy, who glares and rubs his throat but does nothing else, and steps to the center of the room. Surprise, shock, and even a little fear are written on the faces of the observers. The white-tiled walls seem to reflect and magnify these expressions, and from them Sam draws strength and stature. Coldly, he announces: "As long as I'm your Chairman, I don't want to see or hear about *any* drugs, and I don't want any fighting unless it's absolutely necessary. We're going to find more productive ways of using our free time. Otherwise my board and I can make things very uncomfortable for you. Am I understood?" An affirmative murmur ripples through the room. "Good." Sam smiles, letting his eyes crinkle. "Now let's go have some fun."

Trembling with the delayed nervous reaction to his own boldness and trying to hide it, Sam strolls to the counter, retrieves his penguin, and quickly exits.

As the guys follow him back into the concourse, Sam locates a pay phone and digs a quarter out of his pocket. Breathing a little heavily, he dials his own number to check the answering machine for a message from his mother. "Hi there, this is Sam Pauling," crackles his own voice. "No one's home right now, but if you leave your name and number, we'll be sure to call you back maybe if you're lucky. Mom, if that's you, I went to the mall really fast to buy something for Kate. I promise I'll be back real soon. Bye now."

The electronic tone sounds, and Sam punches in a quick series of numbers. He hears the sound of the tape rewinding, then a hollow click as it begins to play. "Hi, Sam, this is Mom. I was just calling to make sure you were all right, and I guess you are. I wish you would've stayed home in bed, but I suppose this errand of yours is pretty important. I'll be home late again, so fix yourself dinner. I really hope you are feeling okay, Sam, and I'm really sorry about last night. I don't know what got into me. I do love you. Goodbye."

Sam hangs up pensively, then rejoins the group. As he reaches them, he senses a new dimension to their joking and laughter, and it makes him uncomfortable. Acutely conscious of their furtive eyes reappraising him, of the hushed, rushed whispers ricocheting around him, he tries to figure out whether it's their respect he has won or their resentment—or a crude mixture of both.

Nymph and the girls rejoin them presently, and the procession sets off for new adventures. As they near one entrance to the mall, whistles and shouted greetings erupt from their mouths. Jen and Moose have just arrived. Sam's eyes lock with Moose's as they approach, and something passes between them, though he isn't sure quite what. "We heard about what you did last night,

Sam," says Jen, her shaved brows wrinkling with the weight of what she wants to say, "what you did for Moose, and I—we—just wanted to thank you for it."

Sam's eyes drop in shame. He hadn't done it for anyone but himself. "Yeah, well, Moose wasn't the guilty one," he says thickly. "Everyone at that party heard Corman make the prediction. We know who was responsible." Nymph squeezes Sam's arm reassuringly, and the crowd makes supportive noises.

Buttressed by this show of solidarity, Sam leads his loose-knit phalanx toward the closest escalator, thinking they can hit the arcades or the theater at the basement level and relax for a while. By two's and three's, they descend, and Sam's eyes and mind wander, soothed and set free by the roaming attention of Nymph's fingers. He enfolds her spontaneously in his arms, idly wondering where he'd be now if he had never met Corman. And as if in answer, a figure glides by them on the escalator up, a girl trying stoically to ignore the downward passage of thirty-odd loud, obnoxious delinquents. Sam stares. "Kate," he says, too loudly, thunderstruck.

She turns—her eyes widen with the shock of recognition. An army of curious faces turn on her as tears poison the beautiful blue pools that have seen so deeply inside of him. A flash of whirling copper, and she dashes up the moving steps, shouldering her way past parcel-laden shoppers.

Sam shrugs Nymph away and darts up through and around and between his crowd of followers, brushing them aside like animalcula of no consequence, stumbling on the descending stairs. Some of the guys try to follow, hoping to watch the fireworks, but none can negotiate the confused wake of people Sam leaves behind in his struggle upward. At last he gains the top, surveys the hustle and bustle, finally spies the telltale mane of copper disappearing into the parking garage. "Kate, wait!" he cries, but when he gets there she is nowhere in sight—no sign of her or of her Rabbit. "Dammit," he hisses, gasping and coughing and holding his side. He forgot how sick he was that morning.

A cool touch on his arm: Nymph tugging with gentle insistence. How could she have followed him through that crowd? "Come on, Sam, let's go back," she coos. "The others—"

Reflexively, without even looking, he backhands her across the face. "Let go of me, bitch." And he stalks angrily to his own car, with the toy penguin locked in a death grip.

XI

TUESDAY EVENING

DEADLY CHILL WHEEZES IN AND OUT OF SAM'S LUNGS. THE porchlight above his head burns steadily, yellow and stained and mottled with dead bugs, although the sun still hovers indecisively above the western horizon. His toes tap a non-rhythm on the cheerful green welcome mat as he rings the doorbell again. The television flickers through the curtains. Someone *has* to be home.

Heavy footsteps, and at last the door swings open, as far as the inside chain will permit. A suspicious face peers through the opening. "What do you want?"

"Uh, hi, Mr. Fitzhugh. I'd like to talk to Kate if I could."

Fitzhugh's lips twist like he's about to spit. "Katie's not home just now."

Sam gestures feebly at the Rabbit parked in the driveway. "But her car's here."

"Listen, didn't you hear me?" The tone grows threatening. "She's not here and won't be until very late. Now go on and beat it." The door slams shut with the finality of a prison cell being locked.

Driving away, Sam catches a glimpse of copper at an upstairs window out the corner of his eye—but when he turns his head for a better look, it's gone.

XII

TUESDAY NIGHT

SAM CRAWLS INTO BED WITHOUT SO MUCH AS A BITE OF DINNER, brushing aside the shattered and unwound cassette tape draped across the sheets. When he arrived home earlier, the first thing he did was rip the tape out of the answering machine and throw it against the wall as hard as he could. It didn't make him feel any better. He reaches across the nightstand for the ouija board and planchette, arranges the items in his lap, and takes a deep breath. "Chet," he says, emotion distilled out of his voice, "what kind of a future have I got with Kate now?"

SAM MY BOY, it spells out—or SAMMY BOY, he can't tell which. Not that it matters. PROPHECIES ARENT THAT EASY TO NE-GATE . . . WHAT I'VE PREDICTED STILL HOLDS . . .

"How? She won't even speak to me."

JUST GO SEE HER AGAIN TOMORROW . . . TAKE THE PENGUIN DOLL . . .

"But what do I tell her? How do I explain what she saw?"

I CANT DO EVERYTHING FOR YOU, it responds condescending-ly. YOULL THINK OF SOMETHING . . . TRUST ME . . .

Sleep, when it comes, sneaks up in fitful snatches, stalks him like a cat. His night divides itself into a sequence of vague, terrifying dream images alternated with wakeful periods of sweat and fear. In one dream, Sam watches in mute horror as Corman shoots Mrs. Finch repeatedly in the stomach, chest, neck, and head. Impossible quantities of rose-red blood cascade to the floor from each wound, like adulterated waterfalls. The woman topples with deliberate grace into a deepening pool of her own fluids. Calmly and with a smug trace of smile, Corman hands Sam the pistol and says: "Now it's your turn, my man."

And Sam takes the weapon, fitted perfectly to his own hand, sights at the prostrate form, fires—once, twice, three times: *bang, bang, bang!* He sinks to his knees, and the blood-level rises to his chest, his chin, his mouth . . .

He wakes with a start, sitting upright in bed, sweat rolling into his eyes, finger pointed at the window like a child's imaginary gun.

Bang!

Pebbles against the glass.

"Bug off, Nymph," he croaks, then flings back the covers and pounds down the stairs. Doesn't she know when to leave well enough alone? Of course she does—but another part of him, one buried deep inside the convolutions of his brain, knows that this is the perfect time for her to come, to get what she craves: punishment. He steps into the yard; she waits in the shadows, her white smudge of makeup a dead giveaway. Accusatorially, he says, "You've got some nerve coming here tonight."

She moves toward him languorously, wraps her arms around his waist; he stands as still as a statue. "I had to come," she purrs, teasing his ear with her lips. "You can't lead them without me— I'm part of the bargain. You *need* me."

Suddenly angry beyond words, he seizes her roughly by the arm and hauls her into the house. Down into the basement, to the unfinished guest bedroom with the bare mattress and the naked light bulb, where he brutally does to her what she so badly wants him to do—what he so badly *needs* to do . . .

XIII

WEDNESDAY MORNING

IT ALL STARTS SIMPLY ENOUGH, INNOCUOUSLY—PREDICTABLY, even. All the chalk removed from the blackboard trays, the students scrambling themselves and rendering the seating chart all but useless: the typical childish games that substitute teachers must learn to put up with. But as five separate voices answer "Here" to Corman's name during roll call, Sam is devising a new kind of game to play.

Mrs. Finch not even two days gone, and everything's proceeding just like she never existed! Not that she was Sam's favorite teacher, but she never hurt anyone—same as him. She didn't deserve to become a victim, and no one had any right to replace her without so much as a word of sorrow. Well, Sam intends to make sure no one forgets what kind of a teacher Agnes Finch really was.

"All right, class," drawls the heavy-lidded, gray-mustachioed substitute, "today I'd like to continue your reading aloud from your textbook on the Greeks. Does someone have the spot marked where we left off yesterday? Hands? Good. You, young lady, in the lavender sweater . . . uh, Kim Black . . . why don't you start for us?"

The students suppress their titters and chuckles. Not only is the real Kim Black sitting in a different seat, but he is also male.

Turns proceed down the row, each person reading a page or so of the text before passing the torch. Sam waits very patiently for his turn to arrive, and just before it does so, halfway through the period, he leans over to the boy next to him and whispers: "Keep a straight face, Harvey. Pass it on."

Harvey looks puzzled, but passes the message as directed. He's a hacker and has faith in Sam.

" '—and thus Athens developed a flourishing trade and an urban civilization.' "

"Fine, thank you," the substitute interrupts. "That's enough. Next, please."

With a shot of adrenaline percolating through his stomach, Sam picks up where the last reader left off. " 'Sparta, on the other hand,' " he reads, " 'developed as a warrior-state. The Spartans had won their land as an invading army, pushing south and enslaving the Mycenaeans. Even when they achieved a relative peace, their military habits were so fixed that they could not be cast off. Spartan boys were conscripted into military training at the age of six, separated from their families, and trained as warriors. As a result of their isolation in barracks, homosexuality was rampant among the males of this city-state.' " He flips suddenly to a random page and continues to read, never missing a beat. " 'In thus emulating the practices of their gods, these men were tagged as blasphemers and exiled, lest judgment from on high should strike down the entire city.' "

The more perceptive students choke back their laughter, while the less perceptive scan their texts in confusion. The substitute flips rapidly through the pages ahead, trying to figure out where he lost the narrative thread. Sam flips the page again and continues:

"'Agriculture became the mainstay of this people's economy, particularly sheep.' Ah"—Sam lowers his head and massages his temples—"my eyes are starting to hurt. Could we please go to the next person?"

The substitute nods curtly, brow furrowed. Behind Sam sits one of the more ambitious guys from the mall yesterday, one who caught on to the sleight-of-mouth immediately. He segues smoothly into the chapter on early Greek heroes—the tale of Odysseus in drag, specifically. Sam smiles to himself. The ball is rolling.

The next student jumps to the chapter on myth, and the next to the pre-Socratic philosophers. Then the narrative jumps right out of the textbook and into Aristophanes's *Lysistrata*. "Ah, people—" begins the substitute, as another student picks up the strand in *Josephus*. "I don't know what—" On to *The Rubáiyát of Omar Khayyám*. "If you think this is amusing—" Into *The Epic of Gilgamesh*. "If this continues, I'm afraid that—" *The Song of Solomon*—the dirty parts. "I don't want to do this—"

The next girl in the rotation departs some distance from the track of classical literature. "'Roughly he grasped her heaving shoulder,'" she reads, "'ripping away the thin material of her shift and forcing her down onto the—'"

The class bursts into hysterics, no longer able to hold back their laughter. "All right, that's quite enough!" roars the substitute, leaping red-faced from his chair. "We'll try this one more time, and if you can't read aloud like well-mannered young men and women, I'll be forced to report you all to the principal. Now . . ."

Still and silent as corpses, the students reopen their textbooks. Sam, staring fixedly into the pages of his book, clears his throat and says: "'It was quiet—too quiet.'"

And the silence shatters.

"That's it! Stay right where you are. I'll be right back—with company." The substitute tries to slam the door on his way out, but it merely hisses shut on its pneumatic hinge.

Sam counts slowly to ten in his head, then rises and opens the door. "Let's go. Out and around the corner, into the ladies' room. Everybody. Quietly. They'll never find us there." He holds the door for them all and, before joining the tail-end of the procession, scrawls a hasty message on the blackboard:

AGNES FINCH LIVES! DEATH TO THE USURPER!

IN CALCULUS THE NEXT PERIOD, SAM LEADS THE BOYCOTT ON A pop quiz. The grading is on a modified curve, where each student is matched against the high score. By default, they all receive A's.

News of his two successful campaigns filter rapidly through the school, and an elite team of disciples flocks to his side, hackers and hipsters alike. As the first-lunch crowds swirl through the hallways, he and his followers descend upon a random empty classroom, where they turn all the desks toward the rear wall, with the exception of the teacher's—which they turn upside-down. Chalked on the wall:

YOU CAN'T CHANGE THE PAST WITH YOUR HEAD UP YOUR ASS! SINCERELY, AGNES' AVENGERS

As they surreptitiously exit, a hand grasps Sam's arm. "What the hell are you doing, man?"

"Leggo of me, Rog," says Sam angrily, shaking his arm.

"No. What were you doing in there?"

"Trying to make a point."

"Oh, yeah? Why not write a letter to the editor instead?"

"Lacks visceral impact."

Roger peers through the doorway. "Agnes' Avengers, huh? You should have been here for the memorial assembly yesterday. You could have had your say without resorting to vandalism."

Sam falters in his anger momentarily. A memorial assembly? Without him there? But that's only one of his crutches; he clings to the other ferociously. "There's more to it than that," he growls. "Did you notice the guys coming out of that room? Half *my* friends, half Corman's, working *together*. There haven't been any fights or incidents today, because I've given them something else to focus their energy on. It's a beautiful thing to see, teamwork."

"Bullshit. Tomorrow they'll be back to the status quo and you'll be yesterday's news."

"Wrong, man. These guys are working together like a well-oiled machine. Tomorrow we'll be *running* this school. By next week we'll be running the whole damn town. Just watch."

Donny Phu materializes out of the mass of students. "Hey, Sam!"

"Donny, my man!" Sam shrugs out of Roger's grasp. "Everything ready?"

A thick bandage covers Donny's temple, and one eye is swollen half shut. "Yeah. The guys are waiting down by the cafeteria. What's keepin' you?"

"Go tell them I'll be right there. Tell them to get in position."

"Right on." Stiffly, Donny disappears into the crowd.

Roger pinches the bridge of his nose. "What are you up to now?"

"Just a small demonstration. Roger, did you *see* that kid? Yesterday he got the shit kicked out of him by a gang of bullies.

Today he's running around having the time of his life with the same guys who beat him up. Don't try to tell me I haven't got something good going here."

"Good, Sam, good. That's really nice. The Great Peacemaker. To tell the truth, I could care less what you're doing with your little buddies. I'm worried about something else. Have you heard the rumors going around? People say you fingered Corman the other night just so you could make off with that nymphomaniac girlfriend of his. And they think you're a friggin' *hero!*"

"Listen, man, those are just ru—"

"I know someone else who's been hearing the rumors. Have you seen Kate at school at all today?"

Sam looks at the floor. "Not actually, no, but—"

"You went and did what you promised you wouldn't do, you bastard. She put all her trust in you, and you threw it back in her face."

"Leave me alone," Sam says softly.

"No!" Roger grabs him by the shoulders and stares him in the eye. "You're making a royal asshole out of yourself, man. I'm not going to stand around and just watch while you turn your life into a goddamn circus!"

"Go to hell!" Sam jerks away violently and melts into the milling throng. Blindly, he lets them push him along, until he no longer knows where he is. A time or two he spies Nymph back in the crowd, but he ducks and changes direction. All thoughts of his cafeteria demonstration are lost to the crowd. He can't even remember what the point was supposed to be.

XIV

WEDNESDAY AFTERNOON

THE DOORBELL CHIMES FAR AWAY, LIKE THE INTERNAL RUMBLING of a giant beast. Sam stands facing away from the door, gazing at the empty driveway. No sign of the candy-apple Rabbit, anywhere. "Who's there?" calls a muffled voice.

"The, uh, UPS man," he stammers. "I've got a package I need you to sign for."

The door opens a crack. Mrs. Fitzhugh's eyes peek around the edge of the door, pale blue replicas of Kate's—though they seem to have lost their piercing quality to some long-ago tragedy. "I wonder what—" She breaks off. "You. I thought my husband told you to stay away."

"Mrs. Fitzhugh, please," says Sam, and he can't keep the desperate edge out of his voice. "I don't know what Kate told you yesterday, but whatever she may have seen was a mistake."

"A big one," she agrees, closing the door.

Sam pulls open the screen, stops the door with his foot. "Please. Kate says you're a compassionate person. Are you going to let both of us go on being hurt just because of a stupid misunderstanding?" When she doesn't answer, Sam presses gently: "Where is she?"

Mrs. Fitzhugh takes a deep breath, avoiding his eyes. Her breasts rise and fall just like her daughter's do, and Sam feels a pang in his heart. "I don't know," she says at last, twisting the little pendant at her throat. "She just said she was going out for a little while, to think. I don't know where she is."

Sam's eyes narrow, focused on the little gold pendant. "Where did you get that?"

"What—this?" She looks down in faint surprise at the pendant. "It's, uh . . . it belongs to Kate. It's a locket I gave her when she was little."

"That's what I thought. What are you doing with it now?"

"What business is—"

"It's *very* important." Sam tries to keep the impatience out of his voice.

She breathes deeply again, and the pang in Sam's heart sharpens. "I'm sorry, Sam. We've all been a little on edge lately. Kate gave this to me this morning, said she wanted me to wear it for a while. She said—"

"Dammit!" Sam hisses, backing down the pathway. "God-*dammit!*" He spins and dashes to his car.

"Sam! Sam, what's the matter? Sam?" Her only answer is the cough and roar of the departing Impala.

He finds her car right where he expected to find it, tucked back between a couple of trees in a far corner of the school parking lot. He brakes to a stop behind it, boxing it in, and kills the engine. The car door flies open and he takes off up the grassy slope. He crests the first hill, surveys the surrounding scrub and brush, then plunges on. By the third hill, his lungs are burning and a sharp lance of pain pierces his side, but these are secondary to the fear welling in his throat. This is further out than she took him before. He presses on.

Over the next hill he spots her. She stands in a gully below, leaning against a tree, like a child counting down for a game of hide-and-seek. Her soft, earthy clothing camouflages her effectively, especially down in the shadows, but her gleaming copper hair gives her away, vivid as a splash of technology against the backdrop of pure virginal forest. He treads softly down the hill, until he stands twenty feet away from her. "Kate," he says gently, just above the threshold of sound.

She doesn't turn away from the tree. "Go away, Sam," she says, her voice thick with unshed tears. "I don't want you here."

"You don't mean that. You wouldn't have come out here if you were trying to hide from me."

Her back straightens, but she remains facing away. "I'm not trying to hide from you, but I don't want you here, either."

Sam takes a few steps closer. "You've been jumping to unfair conclusions. Can't you give me a chance to explain?"

"I don't need to," she says, and her voice hardens. "I know that you become a different person when you're hanging around with your friends. I don't like that other person, Sam, and I refuse to put up with him. And I heard the rumors yesterday at school, about the things that had—had *happened* between you and that slut. I didn't believe them—I *wouldn't* believe them—not until I saw you together for myself."

"She must have started those rumors herself. Listen to me—at the mall yesterday, I wasn't there *with* her. She was harassing me, sexual harassment. Because I put her boyfriend in jail. To her, it was like some kind of a . . . some kind of succession, some kind of inheritance, and she's the prize for whoever knocks the king off Bunker Hill. She won't leave me alone. Don't you see what she's making you do?" He rubs his eyes, then finishes weakly: "She's scaring you off and leaving me defenseless against her, with nothing to fall back on."

"From where I was standing, it looked like she'd gotten through your defenses without any help from me." Her fist clenches, and she holds it in front of her face, studying it. "I'm sorry, Sam. I thought you were the one for a little while there, I really did. I thought you were the one." A trickle of crimson snakes down her forearm, vanishes into the sleeve of her sweater. Her nails, piercing the skin of her hand. "But now I think it would be best if we didn't see each other anymore."

"But Kate—"

"But nothing," she says coldly. "It's over." She spins on her heel and walks away, heading deeper into the woods.

"But Corman said . . . *Chet* said . . . and they're never wrong. You can't just walk away like this! They're never wrong, dammit!"

Her retreating back is as unbending as a steel rod. She doesn't stop.

"Listen to me, Kate! They're never wrong! You're not supposed to be *doing* this!" Sam breaks off suddenly, staring at the back of her head. That's all he has seen this afternoon—the back of her head. Why doesn't she turn around, let him see her face?

Her face. He tries to picture it, but like yesterday, he finds he can't. My God, she's in plain view and I can't even picture her damn *face!* The young woman walking away from him could be *anyone*, wearing any face, and he'd never know it. The swaying hips, the flashing ankles beneath the hem of the long brown cotton wrap-around skirt, the obstinate back, even the coppery hair—they could belong to any of a *thousand* girls, anyone, part of the nameless, faceless horde conspiring to break the two of them apart . . .

"Well, it's not going to work!" Sam runs, setting off after the strange woman into the forest of dappled shadows. Tears of rage sting his eyes, and tears of frustration, blurring his vision. The figure ahead enters deeper shadow, and the image shimmers and shifts like a photograph seen through swirling water. The lines and curves of her form melt, run together, recombine, and Sam recognizes a body he will never forget, never *can* forget. "Why can't you leave me alone?" he screams, and the girl runs faster. "Why do you want to take her away from me?"

The forest is thicker here, and dark green light filters down to the grassy carpet like sand sifting through a complex arrangement of strainers. The girl slides on a patch of black moss, goes down, arms flailing. Sam is on her in a second. "All right, bitch, I've got you now. If you want it so bad, then you're gonna get it!" He pins her to the ground with his weight, stifling her screams with one hand, while the other fumbles roughly for the hem of her skirt. When she tries to bite his fingers, he slaps her so hard that she bruises. Her body relaxes, heaving with uncontrollable sobs. Sam only grows more angry, and he rips away the skirt.

And he does the thing he's been trained to do, the way he's been trained to do it.

THE SUN IS SINKING BEHIND THE HILLS WHEN HE RISES, THE half-naked body at his feet shaking with the pressure of silent sobs. Sam notices the blood for the first time. "Blood," he mouths to himself, eyes large as quarters. There was never any blood before . . .

"Oh, my God!" he cries suddenly, an anguished plea to an ear that isn't listening. He turns and runs the way he came, leaving behind the girl he said he loved. He doesn't stop until he reaches his car. Kate's Rabbit is awash in the blood of the dying sun, swimming in it, drowning. Sam wants away from it, away away *away*. Gasping for air, each breath a new a separate agony, he jumps into his own car, guns the engine, and sends it careening out of the parking lot. Steering with his knees, foot jammed down on the gas, Sam rolls down the window; the blast of cold air that enters seems to sear his lungs, icing them from the inside. His hands tremble. He rolls up the window, but the air stays frigid, so he turns the heater on full.

As he sails through the winding suburban streets, the hot breath of hell spews from the dashboard vents, broiling his brain like a hunk of spitted meat. And one phrase dances with endless variety through its heat-skewed neural pathways:

The board is never wrong. The board is never ever in a hundred thousand years *ever* wrong.

XV

WEDNESDAY NIGHT

THE HOUSE IS EMPTY AND OPPRESSIVE, AND HE PROWLS THROUGH it like a caged animal, up and down the stairs, through every room, with nothing but the dimmest lamps lit. The ouija board sits dormant atop his bed, ignored as studiously as an old man locked away in a rest home. He could ask it how long he has, how much time before they come and haul him away like they hauled Corman away—only two nights ago? Sure, he could find out if he wanted to, but that would take away all the suspense, the suffering, punch a hole in the private little hell he's constructed for himself. No, he could hold out forever if he had to, just so long as the punishment was real—not sugar-coated and alphabet-coded, but *real*.

The phone in his bedroom rings, a strident jangle that slices straight to the core of his brain. He stares at it as it rings again, a third time, and a fourth. He almost doesn't answer it, but he has a feeling that if he doesn't do something about it, it'll just go on ringing forever. He snatches up the receiver, holding it two-fingered, as if it were a snake. "Yeah, what?"

"Where've you been all afternoon, Sam?"

"Roger? What . . . ?"

"I've been trying to call ever since I got home from school. I feel pretty bad about the way I lectured you today."

"You should. Now go to hell and leave me alone."

"I'm trying to say I'm sorry."

"Good for you. Now goodbye."

"What's the matter with you? You should be gloating over this apology, but you're acting like—"

"I said good*bye*, Roger."

"You're not well, man. I'm coming over."

"No, don't— Roger? Shit." Sam slams down the phone. He sits on his bed, face in his hands, and time flows past him like a ponderous, muddy river, with him sitting on the shore, watching it go by. He'll get a confession out of me, he thinks. He always does.

Unguessable eons later, the doorbell rings, and Sam slides back into that great, slow river. Whether it's been five minutes or five hours or five centuries, he can't tell. The bell rings again, but he doesn't move. A fierce pounding ensues, then dies out. Hopefully he's given up and gone away.

"Sam?"

"Shit. That's what I get for not locking the doors," Sam says through his hands. "I thought I told you not to come."

Roger enters the room, moving as silently as a cat, the same way he came through the door and up the stairs. "I had to come. There's something wrong with you. You're not . . . you're not *you* anymore."

"What is this, a conspiracy? Of course I'm me." Sam looks up with an expression of distaste. "Of course I'm fucking *me*. Who the hell do you *think* I am?"

"I don't know," Roger says quietly, pulling a chair out from Sam's desk. "I wish I knew, but I don't."

Sam tries to match Roger's steady gaze, but he fails.

"What's the matter, Sam? Tell me. Maybe I can help." He pauses, one of the awkward kind where no one knows quite what to say. "Are the rumors true?" Roger ventures at last. "About you and that girl, I mean?"

Sam answers viciously. "Does it really matter? I mean, no matter what happened, can you really see me spending the rest of my life with that—that . . ."

"Slut," says Roger helpfully.

Sam doesn't respond for a long time. "Yeah, I guess that's right." He looks up imploringly. "But *can* you?"

Roger starts to say something cutting, but he bites it back. "No," he says instead. "I guess not."

"Then does it really matter whether or not anything happened?"

"Maybe not to some people, maybe not to me . . . but it matters to Kate, and I can sure as hell tell it matters to you." Roger looks down at his shoes. "Have you talked to her—Kate, I mean?"

Suddenly there are tears in Sam's eyes, the distillation of frustration and guilt. "I tried, Rog, I really did. I tried."

"Is that where you were this afternoon?"

Sam nods dumbly. He squeezes his eyes shut, but it doesn't stop the flow of tears.

Roger lifts a hand hesitantly, lets it drop. Then the phone rings, sparing either of them from further action. Sam sniffles and reaches for it, but a loud rattling stays his hand.

"What the hell is that?" Roger says, head swiveling. The planchette is vibrating atop the ouija board like an animal straining to be free of its leash. Roger's eyes widen. "What are you doing with that?"

Sam lays a hand on the pointer, while the phone continues to ring.

"Hey, aren't you going to answer that?"

D . . . O . . . N . . . T . . . A . . . N . . . S . . . W . . . E . . . R . . .

Roger stands up. "Well, if you won't do it, I will."

"Don't."

The ice in Sam's voice merely spurs Roger on. "Damned if I won't." He grabs past Sam and snatches up the receiver. "Hello?"

Sam pulls the handset away from Roger's ear. "Chet said not to, dammit!"

Roger gives Sam a shove that sends him sprawling into the corner, and Sam just lies there whimpering, all resistance drained away. He hears the mumble of a voice somewhere far away, whispering past like the muddy river that has once more deposited him upon its banks. The water trickles by with no particular haste, until, years later, they rise and sweep him away again . . .

"Sam?"

He looks up blankly as the figure above him swims into focus. It's Roger, the phone dangling from his hand like a dead animal. "Rog . . . ?"

"That was your mother," says Roger quietly, with distant eyes, a distant voice. "Kate slashed her wrists a little while ago. She just died in the emergency room."

THEY FOUND HER AT HOME, IN THE BATHTUB, ROGER RELAYS. No note—just a lot of blood. They got her to the hospital as fast as they could, but it wasn't fast enough.

Sam feels his stomach trying to consume itself. She had driven home first—removed him from the scene of the incident. She had protected him, even after what he had done. He didn't deserve it.

A chill goosesteps down the skin of his back, sinking into his spinal cord and riding his nervous system like a subway vigilante. He stumbles downstairs, sets about building a fire in the old fireplace that hasn't seen a flame for years. He finds matches, some old newspapers for kindling, and an ancient Duraflame log, like the ones his father could never light. A crackling blaze is soon dancing in the little alcove.

As Sam carefully draws the screen across the fireplace, muttering phrases about the cold, Roger pads silently down the stairs. "There's something I didn't tell you," he says.

"What?" Sam dusts off his hands, throws himself down like a bearskin rug before the fire.

"Your mother says the doctor thinks Kate was sexually assaulted a little while before she killed herself."

"Sexually assaulted," Sam repeats tonelessly. "Is that what they call it?"

"That's the nice way to say it. Would you rather they said rape?"

"Why do you sound so accusatory?"

"Accusatory? I'm not being accusatory. Not unless—" Roger pales. "My God, Sam. You didn't."

Sam springs to his feet. "It wasn't my goddamn *fault!*" he screams. "I *had* to do it! There was nothing else I could do!"

Roger folds his arms across his chest, trembling with something barely contained. The flickering firelight draws golden highlights out of his hair. "What the hell do you mean?"

"It had to happen *some*how!" Sam stamps his foot with the emphasis, his face twisting like a clay-animation model. "It was predicted!"

"Who predicted it?" asks Roger with seething calm.

"Chet did, dammit!"

Roger lifts an eyebrow in question.

"He's my fucking ouija board!"

"Not the ouija board again. Don't tell me you let Corman talk you into believing that crap."

"It's *true*," Sam whines. "It predicted I'd concede the chess match, it predicted Mrs. Finch's murder, and it predicted—"

"It predicted a roll in the hay for you and Kate, and you *believed* the damn thing because that's exactly what you wanted to hear! A piece of wood can't predict the future, Sam! It just spells out whatever's in your subconscious!"

"No, not when twelve people—"

"I don't care what kind of proof you thing you have—it's all bullshit. It tells you something you want to hear, and when it looks like it's never gonna happen, you go ahead and make it happen anyway! You . . . you—" Roger breathes deep and finishes in a vicious whisper: "You *raped* her!" He turns abruptly and mounts the stairs.

Roger's accusations have fallen like shackles around Sam's body. "Where are you going?" he says in a small voice.

"I'm gonna do what you should have done at the earliest possible moment." Roger disappears into Sam's room. "I'm getting rid of this thing for you."

"No!" Sam shrieks, charging up the stairs. "You can't! I won't know what to do! I won't know how to lead my men!"

Roger emerges from Sam's bedroom with the ouija board clamped firmly in both hands. "You're gonna lead them right into jail or hell or into whichever one wants to take you first."

An involuntary grin quirks across Sam's face, and he plunges into the bedroom and scoops up the planchette, which Roger neglected. Then he follows him into the living room, where Roger kneels at the hearth and stokes up the fire. "You don't know what you're doing," Sam says calmly from the foot of the staircase.

"You can't stop me," Roger asserts. "Once this thing is gone, you won't have any scapegoat to blame things on. You'll have to accept the responsibility for your own actions. I'm doing you a favor."

"Undoubtedly," says Sam smugly.

The front door creaks open slowly, and Nymph pokes her head through the gap. "Sam?" she says tentatively, then notices Roger at the hearth. She darts into the room and shuts the door behind her. "Sam, what's he doing?"

"Is that that little slut-friend of yours?" Roger says with a sneer. "Well, she can watch, too." And he adds another wad of newspaper to the blaze, then drops the ouija board on top. Sparks and ashes fly in all directions, and little tongues of flame lick around its edges.

Nymph throws her arms around Sam's waist and buries her face against his shoulder. "For God's sake, what's he *doing?*"

Sam draws her into the kitchen. The planchette begins to dance in his hand, as if tiptoeing across hot coals. "Nymph," he says gently, "don't worry. I've got Chet right here." He pats the pointer, then seats her at the kitchen table. "He's the important thing. The board itself doesn't really matter." But the planchette's vibration intensifies.

Sam sits down and Nymph takes his hands across the polished Formica tabletop. "Sam, I've got to talk to you," she says in a very small voice. Her fancy makeup is missing, and tears have etched twin streaks of mascara down her cheeks. Her hair is disheveled, and her provocative dress rumpled. Her eyes peer out from sunken, hollow sockets, red from crying. "I just found out about Kate, what . . . happened to her." She sniffles. "I'm so sorry. I didn't know what was going to happen or I could have stopped it."

A lump rises in Sam's throat. "What do you mean?" he says huskily. The pointer clatters wildly on the tabletop.

Nymph's words are punctuated by tears and shuddering breaths. "If it wasn't for me, you couldn't have done what you did to her. You wouldn't have known how." Her eyes fall; the tears won't stop. "I taught you how to rape, and now a very beautiful girl is dead, a girl you loved. I'm so sorry, I just don't know—"

The last sentence dissolves into weeping, and Sam leaves his chair to cradle her in his arms, smoothing her hair and trying to murmur soothing things into her ear. But he can't, because he is crying just as hard as she. Through his tears, he asks, "Why did you do it?"

"Because of Chet. I couldn't help it. He—he'd do things for me if I did what he wanted. If I didn't, he'd—" She screams in sudden agony, as if illustrating the point she wanted to make.

At the same moment, Roger enters the kitchen, sooty and smiling. And at the same moment, the planchette stops moving—and its voice speaks directly into Sam's head:

—Put her out of her misery, boy. She's suffering, and you don't need her anymore.

"Chet?" he says in confusion.

Roger rushes to the table. "What's the matter with her, Sam?"

—She admitted it was her fault that Kate died. Kill her.

"Chet, I thought you—"

The screams continue, and Nymph's body writhes like a fish on dry land. Roger tries to hold her down, while Sam stares at the wall. "Dammit, Sam, what's wrong with her?"

—Your so-called friend there just destroyed the only thing that was keeping me bound. The board was the circuit, the step-down transformer. Without it, you get a powerful arc of current straight from my mind to yours. And now I can tell you that you must kill this girl, Sam, before she hurts you any worse than she already has.

Roger shakes him violently by the shoulders. "What the hell is wrong with her? What have you done to her?" Nymph's screams fill the background like a police siren.

"She told me you made her do it!"

—Of course she would, but I couldn't have done anything to coerce her while I was still confined. You have to kill her or her deceit will kill you.

Sam claps his hands to his ears, but he can't shut out the unearthly voice that fills his head. "What are you doing to her?" he screams.

Roger flings Sam away in disgust and tries to restrain Nymph. "I'm trying to help her, you bastard!"

—I'm doing nothing, I *can* do nothing. She's epileptic. She's having a seizure, and her reflexes are very strong. You'll have to kill her before she hurts your friend.

"*No!*"

"Shut up!"

—You *will*.

Sam stands, jerkily, against his will, limbs flailing like those of a marionette. He walks to the cupboard in stop-motion, reaches for his mother's big carving knife. Chet's presence fills his mind, his soul, his fingers and toes—and suddenly Sam knows what it feels like to be violated, what it feels like to be raped.

His mind recoils in horror.

His fingers curl around the handle of the knife, slowly contracting, like a delicate, supernaturally operated waldo. The varnished wood caresses his palm, his fingers, with a cool, smooth kiss. It fits his hand perfectly. "Stop it, you lying bastard!" With a convulsive shudder, Sam drops the knife and runs, snatching the planchette from the tabletop. He stumbles to his knees in front of the hearth. The ouija board is no more than a loosely connected film of ash spread over the coals. With planchette in hand, he tries to reach into the fireplace, but it's like punching through a wall of tar. The muscles of his arm, his back, strain and crack with the effort. His fingers are clenched about the pointer as tightly as ribbed steel bands, and they won't open. He pries at them with his other hand, peeling them away one at a time, until the object lies free on his open palm.

And he drops it into the fire.

A scream reverberates inside his head, a chilling, tormented thing that never originated in this world. It tears at his brain with the jagged edge of a rip saw. Then something hot smacks Sam in the face, and the unearthly shriek dies. His eyes sting, and he paws them open. The planchette sits before him on the rug, charred but whole. A drop of blood from his nose spatters on the leg of his pants. The planchette bounds past him under its own volition, toward the kitchen doorway.

Sam twists his body. The pointer leaps like a little dirt-brown toad. He throws himself on it, feels the sharp end dig into his chest, wrestles it into his hands, and rolls back to the hearth. This time he plunges the planchette into the middle of the flames with both hands and holds it there, arms and shoulders straining. The demonic scream erupts once more inside his head, only now, it blends with his own until the two become one. Tongues of flame curl around his hands, blistering the flesh and turning it black. The fire enters his body through his palms, like air sucked into a vacuum, races along his nerves like electric current and turns his bones to powdery ash. The arcs of flame converge in the middle of his chest, then fan out to immolate every cubic inch of his body. His reflexes scream for him to let go, but he won't.

The blaze collects in the pit of his stomach, growing, throbbing, crackling, until his body can no longer contain it. A jet of flame lances out of him like a bolt of lightning, punching straight through the wall and into the kitchen. It knocks Roger away and seizes Nymph in its fiery fist, lifts her like a rag doll. Sam sees the scene in his mind, the girl's body being invaded and animated by fire. The orange-yellow conflagration burns behind her eyes, and deep crimson flames spout from the crown of her head to curl down around her face, neck, and shoulders like a burning wig. She blinks, and her smoke-black irises glow suddenly blue, the intense, piercing blue of eastern sky just before dawn. "Let it go, Sam," she says, her voice the dry crackle of burning leaves, "and we can bring her back to you." The crimson flames about her head seem to crystalize into flowing strands of fine copper wire.

The image sickens him. "No!" he shrieks, and the apparition's skin begins to bubble and run like melting plastic. Burning liquid dribbles to the floor, where it hardens into a smoldering mound. Muscle and sinew unravel beneath the flow of skin, and hot blood boils away into the air. The eyes pop and run like cracked eggs. Gradually, the fire strips the body clean, until nothing remains but charred bones encasing a live and beating heart. The blaze contracts about it like a fist, squeezes, and it bursts.

The fire disappears, the bones clatter to the floor, and Sam rolls onto his back, feeling a future of glory trickle through his ruined fingers like fine ash.

AND LATER, IN HIS HOSPITAL BED, HANDS TIED DOWN AND smeared with salve, the pre-dawn light fills two small windows with color—windows which gaze down upon him like a pair of benevolent and forgiving sky-blue eyes.

www.ingramcontent.com/pod-product-compliance
Lightning Source LLC
Chambersburg PA
CBHW022038170626
46808CB00003B/1265